ANOTHER
WORLD

CLASHING REVELATIONS TRILOGY: BOOK 2

ANOTHER
WORLD

I.M. STOICUS

Paperback ISBN: 978-1-63337-794-3
Hardback ISBN: 978-1-63337-795-0
E-book ISBN: 978-1-63337-796-7

ANOTHER WORLD is dedicated to the **I. M. Stoicus'** loving and caring mother-in-law, who turned eighty in March of 2024. She has given the author and others genuine motherly love and respect. Along with her wise husband, she permitted **I. M. Stoicus** to marry their precious and beautiful daughter. That permission has produced over twenty-four years of marriage, which has begotten two remarkable sons. His mother-in-law has consistently demonstrated the love and unity required for her entire family. These few words sincerely express the author's and his family's appreciation towards her: 我们爱你, we love you. Mom, your caring and honorable actions encourage us to adhere to God's commandment from Deuteronomy 5:16: *"Honour thy father and thy mother, as the Lord thy God hath commanded thee; that thy days may be prolonged, and that it may go well with thee, in the land which the Lord thy God giveth thee."*

1.

DISCOVERED SALVATION

CAPTAIN GOMEZ WAS FIGHTING FOR HIS LIFE in a foxhole in Africa in February of 2097, so he radioed his commander. "Sir, we are engaged in an unbelievably fierce attack. Our **Area of Operation (AO)** is occupied with belligerents, soulless HUNTERS. All enemy combatants have only small-arm weapons. There are no noncombatants or civilians. At least nine HUNTERS and thirty enemy HUNTERBOTS are detected. They are approximately one hundred meters northeast of **OBJECTIVE RESCUE,**" Captain Gomez reported. HUNTERBOTS were lethal AI robots that were under the control of the HUNTERS; the HUNTERS were ruthless satanic soldiers of the tyrannical **UTOPIAN KINGDOM.**

Back at battalion headquarters, which was located at base camp, Lieutenant Colonel Solon responded, "We fired artillery rounds toward the stated enemy's location. Take cover. Be aware; danger close."

Lieutenant Colonel Solon heard the devastating artillery rounds explode; he was two kilometers from the fighting. These overwhelming blasts rocked the ground like a horrendous earthquake. This combative encounter was merely one of at least five other deadly engagements that his dedicated battalion was currently fighting in the central part of Africa; Solon's battalion had 888 soldiers. Solon pondered to himself about the meaning of Psalm 23:4: *"Yea, though I walk through the valley of the shadow of death, I will fear no evil: for thou art with me; thy rod and thy staff, they comfort me."*

Captain Gomez radioed, "That is a bullseye. That was the third one today. It was a direct hit, sir. Empire HUNTERS are neutralized. There are no survivors or functional enemy HUNTERBOTS. There is good news. Company LIBERATION has no casualties. Sir, we recommend moving out to support Company ALPHA OMEGA, which is only two kilometers away."

Lieutenant Colonel Solon responded, "That is outstanding and a brilliant recommendation. Move out to assist Company ALPHA OMEGA. They are currently skirmishing against a company-size unit of bloodthirsty HUNTERS with numerous HUNTERBOTS; we estimate 140 total enemy personnel. They have at most three armored vehicles. I shall send eight hovercrafts immediately to neutralize the armored vehicles. Continue sending updates and required spot reports every fifteen minutes. Advance with Godspeed."

Captain Gomez thought to himself, *War is hell! However, I must keep my focus and stay in the present. As Marcus Aurelius, the last historic Roman Emperor of the Pax Romana, stated: "You have power over your mind—not outside events. Realize this, and you will find strength." Furthermore, Lieutenant Colonel Solon has made sure that our back is covered. I trust his judgment and strategic assessments.*

Captain Gomez, one of Solon's most dedicated officers, has served with him for over three years; he was an exceptional combat engineer officer and a sapper. Moreover, he was a natural-born human raised by his parents in a hidden city. Solon, on the other hand, was a biologically and technologically Artificially Enhanced

(AE) HUMAN. Solon was able to have downloaded software placed into him, and additionally, he possessed unbelievable strength and endurance. Solon, thanks to his deceased parents, was enhanced significantly more than any other AE HUMAN. His developmental time was approximately 666 days from conception to adult per se. He had only nine additional days to be trained to be an officer in the military in a dystopian empire; however, he was clearly a lean, mean fighting machine. On the other hand, his parents ensured that his love of humanity was maintained.

HUNTERS were Artificially AE HUMANS from the **UTOPIAN KINGDOM**. The **UTOPIAN KINGDOM** was the result of combining the two former empires, **the Germanic Nazi EMPIRE** and **the Rising Sun Maoist EMPIRE**. The demonic and tyrannical **UTOPIAN KINGDOM** seems to be in a proxy war with the developing **FEDERAL REPUBLIC**. Furthermore, these developed countries are currently the only two functional nations in the world; these two nations have an effective, stable government and a formative military. The rest of the world's developing nations had less than a few million people and ineffective governments and militaries.

Captain Gomez stated, "Sir, we have reached our objective. We are currently fighting with a seasoned hostile HUNTER platoon of approximately thirty to forty personnel. Company Alpha Omega is outflanking them with speed and success."

Lieutenant Colonel Solon reacted, "That is magnificent. Armored hovercrafts should be in your AO."

Captain Gomez replied, "Yes, Sir. Our kickass hovercrafts and drones have eliminated the nemesis's armored vehicles. Your hovercrafts are now eliminating the HUNTER platoon personnel.

It is like fishing with dynamite in a barrel. It reminds me of when I was fishing illegally back home with my dad. I love being a country boy."

Lieutenant Colonel Solon responded, "That is extremely impressive. Maintain great performance and continue fishing with dynamite. Do you all need any artillery support or medical support?"

Captain Gomez answered, "Sir, there is no necessity for artillery for now; however, we desperately need medical assistance for the prisoners of war. We have neutralized the enemy. We have three prisoners with no injuries and six injured prisoners. There are nine prisoners of war and twenty-seven de-inactivated enemy HUNTERBOTS. We interrogated their highest-ranking officer and retrieved intel from enemy HUNTERBOTS. We have acquired the suspected location of a HUNTER'S Battalion. The supposed location of the enemy unit is fifteen kilometers northeast of **OBJECTIVE RESCUE.**"

Lieutenant Colonel Solon replied, "Medical Company HOPE shall send two squads of medical personnel to your position. Ensure that enemy HUNTERBOTS are sent to the AI Conversion Platoon. You all have performed your assignments extremely well. Be aware that higher command has directed energy weapons, DEW, covering your area. Contact higher with your given code if you have an approved target. Remember to have exact coordinates." AI Conversion Platoon converted and repurposed robots to fight for the **FEDERAL REPUBLIC.** In addition, Lieutenant Colonel Solon sent surveillance combat drones to the probable location of HUNTER'S Battalion. Captain Gomez's intel was dead on. Lieutenant Colonel ordered heavy artillery and DEW on the aforementioned position. The enemy battalion was utterly obliterated, with no survivors. Sixty-six HUNTERS and six hundred enemy HUNTERBOTS were discovered dead or destroyed, which was verified via the surveillance drones; this was a typical enemy-sized battalion of 666 personnel or AI robots.

Solon pondered, *As Sun Tzu revealed: "In warfare, there are no constant conditions. He who can modify his tactics in relation to his opponent will succeed and win." We have modified our tactics to safeguard success. My soldiers execute with precision and effectiveness.*

Major Williams informed, "Sir, we captured an additional eleven hostile HUNTERS; our approved requested DEW destroyed with deadly precision thirty-three enemy HUNTERBOTS and a HUNTER platoon-sized element, approximately forty soldiers or robots. Furthermore, we rescued thirty-three innocent non-combatants and civilians. All civilians and prisoners of war do not need any medical assistance. However, we definitely require transportation assets."

Lieutenant Colonel Solon replied, "That is terrific work. I am sending eight armored transport hovercrafts with Military Police, MPs, to your location. Expect them to arrive in ten minutes."

Major Williams pondered, *As Samurai Miyamoto Musashi's two quotes revealed: "Do nothing that is of no use" and "Think lightly of yourself and deeply of the world." These two quotes inspired me to stay focused on our mission: defeating the enemy and saving civilians.* Major Williams was Solon's right-hand man and executive officer, an exceptional logistical officer with a quartermaster background. He had been with Solon for over three years and was an AE HUMAN.

Captain Smith of Company HOUND DOGS informed, "Sir, we may have found the hidden city of **SALVATION**. There are tens of thousands of non-combatants in this discovered miraculous cave system. It is a well-hidden underground civilization. Oh, thank the good Lord. Sir, there are people from all walks of life. There are magnificent domestic and wild animals, too. It looks like the Garden of Eden. The location is eight kilometers north of **OBJECTIVE RESCUE**. I am sending the exact location in our secret code through the mission-given alternate net."

There was now a ceasefire with Solon's battalion, which was in complete control and was victorious over the HUNTERS. Lieutenant Colonel Solon responded, "That is terrific. I shall be at your position in fifteen mikes." 'Mikes' was military slang for minutes. Solon pondered to himself, *As revealed in Luke 18:27: "And he said, The things which are impossible with men are possible with God." The Lord may have demonstrated another miracle and blessing for humanity by discovering the underground city named SALVATION.* **SALVATION** was one of many hidden cities; however, the remarkable underground city was one of the largest and most advanced.

Solon ordered his dedicated unit, named BATTALION DAGGER, to secure the AO. He reported to his commander, Brigadier General Apollo, and his headquarters. General Apollo reminded him of the importance of finding additional humans, since HUNTERS were hunting them down, and the importance of reviving the human race with genuine humans, since most AE HUMANS were sterile. Furthermore, he stated that his unit required reinforcements from medical support to transportation assistance to additional security units. In addition, they had achieved the primary mission.

Brigadier General Apollo replied, "Your request is granted and will be handled immediately. We pray that your dedicated unit has found the so-called mystifying city of **SALVATION**. I also plan to meet you there in sixty mikes with your requested support."

Lieutenant Colonel Solon arrived at the alleged **SALVATION** with his entourage. The medical unit assessed the discovered humans, who seemed appreciative of the medical support. Lieutenant Colonel encountered a young lady. He said, "Hello, please assist me in meeting your leader or leaders."

The young girl responded, "You do not look like a demonic elite, HUNTER, or a vanguard. You look like an honorable, trustworthy soldier. Please follow me; however, you do not need your weapons of war. We are a peaceful people." Lieutenant Colonel Solon left his weapons with his security detail and had four soldiers do the same. They followed the kind young lady and met an elderly man who had a wise presence.

The elderly man expressed, "Welcome to our city, **SALVATION**. I have been monitoring your military engagements with the HUNTERS. Thank you for eliminating the enemy. As you are probably aware, the enemy is able to bypass our cloaking devices; thus, they know where we are. Is it true that you have succeeded in your revolution against the evil tyrannical elites?"

Lieutenant Colonel Solon responded, "Yes, we have successfully liberated two empires; we liberated their respective vital cities, like **Utopianapolis,** over a year ago. The former Aztec Empire and Federal Republic Empire are united and are in the process of developing a **FEDERAL REPUBLIC** with a constitution. This unification is extremely remarkable since these nations used to be enemies in an endless, meaningless war against each other.

"Unfortunately, the newly created **UTOPIAN KINGDOM** has become the next so-called utopian empire. Of course, the satanic elites, vanguards, and czars ruled the **UTOPIAN KINGDOM**. We have been in a cold war with them for the same period. The czars have had no desire to have peace talks or diplomatic relationships with us."

The wise man responded, "This confirms our intel. I assume you are the famous Lieutenant Colonel Solon, the *Liberator*, and your Brigadier General Apollo is the heroic *Enforcer*. I am extremely honored to meet you and look forward to meeting Brigadier General Apollo. I am Elder Thales. My ultimate desire is my people's safety, well-being, and liberation. Some of us have been in this cave system for over seventy years. This hidden city is the headquarters of hundreds of other hidden cities; you are aware of numerous other hidden cities since you and others have already saved several million people."

The hidden cities were being discovered by the **UTOPIAN KINGDOM** ever since they developed a new technology that penetrated the hidden cities, cloaking defensive systems. Moreover, the lion's share of the hidden cities had no military protection or fighting capabilities.

Elder Thales continued, "Please be aware that practically everyone is a biologically born human with no enhancements. However, some AE HUMANS escaped from the so-called utopian cities. Ironically, some former vanguards and elites have found their souls and been hiding with us. To ease your concerns, these individuals have all been here for over fifty years. These individuals could not support what the elite utopian empires were becoming or became."

Elder Thales had been one of the critical elders of **SALVATION** for the last five years; this devoted sage was clearly one of the cognoscenti. Elder Thales was in his last year of serving as an elder. Each hidden city had three elders to oversee the executive and judiciary duties. There was a council of twelve councilpersons to create laws and determine taxes and budgets. These councilpersons were elected for two years with no term limits. The three elders were chosen by the councilpersons to serve a one-time six-year term; however, an elder could be elected as councilperson after his or her tenure was served. These twelve councilpersons select an elder every two years since an elder served for a six-year term and all three elders were appointed at a different time. Elder Thales thought, *I am striving to live by Mahatma Gandhi's quote: "The best way to find yourself is to lose yourself in the service of others." I thank the good Lord for saving this hidden city. The people of SALVATION need to have life, liberty, and the pursuit of happiness without tyranny.*

They continued to have cordial and informative conversations. As they were about to tour the remarkable and unbelievable underground city, Brigadier General Apollo arrived. Brigadier General Apollo introduced himself, and they proceeded to tour the enormous city. They were amazed at how well-lit the underground city was. They revealed that everything was powered by geothermal energy or nuclear power. There were numerous greenhouses for growing a variety of fruits and vegetables. In addition, there were a significant number of types of animals for the purposes of ranching, being domesticated pets, and being part of the beautiful natural landscape. Solon and Apollo saw house-trained dogs and cats for the first time. Furthermore, they saw beasts of burden, like cattle and donkeys, as well.

The city of **SALVATION** was an advanced technological city; there were automatic street cleaners, domestic AI robots, and SERVICEBOTS; these technologies ensured that everything remained spotless and orderly. The lighting was impressive since its illumination was equivalent to the sun.

As Solon and others were touring **SALVATION**, the local people were friendly and managed their shops and businesses. As Solon passed a Chinese restaurant, **DRAGON DELIGHT**, he saw a sign to celebrate the Chinese New Year, which was today: February 12, 2097, the beginning of the Chinese Year of the Snake.

A curious German shepherd puppy seemed fond of Solon, especially when Solon picked him up and petted him. This encounter was the first time that he had ever held a puppy. The Elder Thales stated, "This precious, adorable puppy seems to have become very attached to you. I shall tell my beloved wife that this adorable puppy is yours now. We have been trying to give a few away."

Brigadier General Apollo laughed with pure delight. He spoke, "Solon, go for it. The loveable puppy likes you." Solon just beamed and embraced the affectionate puppy with a childlike affection. They continued their informative tour. Apollo declared, "Elder Thales, we must extract everyone to our country for your people's safety and freedom."

Elder Thales responded, "I concur since the HUNTERS would soon know of our location and existence. Besides, as you are aware, the UTOPIAN KINGDOM penetrated our cloaking system a few months ago. I shall obtain the council's approval as well as the concurrence of the other two elders. I doubt that anyone would disagree.

"Be aware that we have several million people in this city and other cities, from babies to senior citizens, with at least tenfold animals of all kinds. In addition, we have libraries of information that must come with us. We have numerous individuals who spent their entire lives in professions that were deemed illegal or unworthy by the elites. These unworthy professions are priests, rabbis, teachers, entertainers, historians, philosophers, mothers, fathers, and a plethora of others."

Brigadier General Apollo radioed the situation to the military headquarters; he informed them that **OPERATION ARK** had started. Apollo ordered Solon to secure the **SALVATION** AO, as well as to continue to pursue the HUNTERS. In addition, he ordered the satellite units to protect **SALVATION** with DEW coverage and surveillance.

As Brigadier General Apollo and Lieutenant Colonel Solon departed from the immense cave system, Solon saw some HUNTERS in the distance who were about to attack. Apollo, unfortunately, was paying attention to Elder Thales, who was still in the cave. Solon shoved Apollo out of the way; he shot a HUNTER and a HUNTERBOT with his automatic rifle; these deadly foes were approximately thirty meters away. He ordered his soldiers to secure the area and track down the other two combative HUNTERS that he saw in the distance.

Brigadier General Apollo cautiously arose from the ground. He stated, "Solon, thanks again. I think that this is the third time that you have saved my life. One of these days, I must return the favor, my friend. I shall get out of here in order to obtain your crucial reinforcements, as well as to strive to get other needed assets approved." Apollo thought, *Aristotle was correct: "Friendship is essentially a partnership." I am incredibly fortunate to have Solon as a friend and a comrade in arms. To show my appreciation, I shall surprise him in the future with an unexpected largess. Besides, I must admit that Solon is like a brother to me.*

Solon responded, "Sir, please take my heartwarming puppy to the rear." Apollo grinned and told a sergeant to secure the puppy.

Brigadier General Apollo replied, "My brother in arms, I owe you tremendous gratitude. I look forward to returning this adorable puppy to you when you return to **Utopianapolis**. Take care and Godspeed."

Solon thought to himself, *Well, I gained a companion. I now have a pet and a new member of the family.*

Solon's dedicated soldiers captured the two HUNTERS. These prisoners of war were sent to a holding area to be processed and sent to the rear. Furthermore, several other minor skirmishes occurred with few casualties. Brigadier General Apollo successfully obtained additional assets and personnel for Solon's units.

For the next few months, the extraction of the people of **SALVATION** happened flawlessly. The **FEDERAL REPUBLIC** forces created and developed a sophisticated air defense system. Practically every day, incoming enemy artillery rounds or rockets tested the air defense system to its limits. Unfortunately, there was a deadly rocket strike that killed several thousand people. Unfortunately, one of the deadly rockets exploded a few hundred meters from Solon. Regrettably, Solon was seriously injured since he did not take cover. He shielded a young girl with his body from the blast. Fortunately, the young girl was not injured; however, Solon was unconscious and barely alive. The paramedics arrived and immediately sent him to the rear for medical attention. During his absence, Major Williams, his executive officer, was placed in charge as the acting battalion commander.

Solon's injuries were extremely grave, and he was placed in a medically induced coma. He had shrapnel in both his right leg and right arm, as well as a concussion. A devoted nurse from **SALVATION** was assisting the wounded; one of her patients was Solon. Her name was Nurse Mei. She was monitoring his progress with true dedication and amazement; she was astonished since he was an AE HUMAN with unknown, highly sophisticated enhancements. It was evident that Solon was more than a typical AE HUMAN; his body had an unbelievable ability to restore itself. Solon did not scar; his body repaired any tissue damage; his injured kidney also regenerated into a fully functional kidney in a matter of days.

As Solon was in his coma, he was dreaming these thoughts. *I may be dying, or I may be dead. I do not know. Unfortunately, I do not have any family since Czar Dolos and others murdered my parents. I feel completely abandoned and empty. Nevertheless, I must remember that I have friends and comrades in the military; however, it is not the same. I do not consider them loved ones, yet they are genuinely brothers and sisters in arms.*

I do not know if I am in heaven or hell or merely in a state of limbo. I am haunted and mesmerized by the last words that Jesus stated on the cross from Mathew 27:46: "And about the ninth hour Jesus cried with a loud voice, saying, 'Eli, Eli, lama

sabachthani?' *That is to say, 'My God, my God, why hast thou* *forsaken me?'"*

Solon heard a pleasant, angelic voice of inspiration and encouragement. After being in a coma for several days, Solon finally opened his eyes. He believed that he saw a beautiful heavenly angel; however, he quickly realized that that angel was a welcoming, gorgeous nurse.

Nurse Mei stated, "Welcome back to the conscious world, soldier; it is still 2097; the date is May 18, 2097. You have been in a coma for five days. You are probably starving and dehydrated. If you are able and willing, I will have food and drinks for you. However, I understand if you wish to wait to eat or drink." Solon smiled and nodded. He ate and drank like a famished tiger, which entertained Nurse Mei. She just smiled with delight since he had his appetite and could keep his food down. Nurse Mei was a very dedicated nurse who truly cared for and sympathized with her patients.

After a few days, Nurse Mei informed, "Lieutenant Colonel Solon, your injuries are healing exponentially. Obviously, your enhancer did an exceptional job working on you. I saw your unbelievable medical records. If you were a human like me, I'd recommend at least six weeks or more of hospitalization. However, your injuries are healing exceptionally well and exponentially.

"Furthermore, thank goodness, there is no brain damage from your ugly incident. Thus, your doctor has concurred that you will only need three more days in the hospital. I am extremely happy for you. Your required rehabilitation time at the hospital will end soon." Mei thought to herself, *I hope that my feelings* *are not so obvious. Solon is a handsome six-foot-tall man with* *gorgeous brown eyes, who is exceptionally muscular, without an ounce of fat. He has beautiful dark hair and brown skin. His enhancer did an exceptional job.*

Solon spoke, "Nurse Mei, thank you for all your medical care. Please tell me where my uniform and other things are."

Nurse Mei innocently responded, "I washed and ironed your clothes for you. I neatly folded them in the dresser."

Solon stated, "Thank you. You are a Godsend. I deeply appreciate all that you have done for me. You are an outstanding nurse. By the way, do you know where you shall be stationed?"

She smiled teasingly. She responded, "Yes, I will be close to where you are stationed in **Utopianapolis**." She left a note on the desk, a beautifully handwritten message with all her contact information; there was a red heart in the corner of the note with a Chinese character, *ji de*, in the heart. The Chinese character *ji de* is translated *to remember*. She also suggested in the note that he should name his curious puppy HERO.

That night, Solon thought to himself in his medical bed, *Well, I thank the Lord for my puppy and meeting Nurse Mei. God has not abandoned me. These relationships relieve me from feeling utterly alone since I am an orphan now; however, I still miss my parents. Moreover, Mei is right. My puppy's name will be HERO.*

I do not know what to think of Nurse Mei. However, she reminds me of several of the beautiful qualities of my beloved mother, Aphrodite. Mei is sweet, humorous, very mysterious, and highly feminine. I pray that she is as devoted to God as my mother was. Nurse Mei is the first woman that I find extremely attractive and am willing to take a chance with. So far, my parents would have approved of her. I truly do.

Solon pulled out his Saint Michael medal that his mother had given him and a Bible he had found on one of his combat missions. He read several chapters from the gospel of Matthew and Psalms. He concentrated on Psalm 117: "*O praise the LORD, all ye nations: praise him, all ye people. For his merciful kindness is great toward us: and the truth of the LORD endureth for ever. Praise ye the LORD.*"

Brigadier General Apollo came to check on Solon. He presented Solon with a heroic medal, the second-highest medal; he earned an additional medal, the third award of this kind, for his valiant injury; this meant that he had injuries from at least three separate courageous events. Brigadier General Apollo stated, "Thank you again for saving my life, my friend. By the way, your unit is doing extremely well. They expressed their concerns for you and look forward to your return, especially Major Williams." Brigadier General Apollo gave Solon a bottle of vintage white wine as a gift, and a copy of a video of his parents' trial, which Solon insisted on viewing. They talked for a couple of hours about everything from his parent's trial to Nurse Mei. Brigadier General Apollo emphasized that his parents were heroes, and our new nation should honor them as such. Solon was speechless and trying to avoid being emotional. Moreover, Brigadier General Apollo informed him of their new nation's progress; he informed him that the delegates were debating over constitutional law and rights. They clearly needed assistance in understanding historical and philosophical reasoning to resolve their gridlocks.

Before leaving, Brigadier General Apollo stated, "By the way, your puppy, HERO, is safe in **Utopianapolis** under the care of AI Thirteen. In addition, AI Thirteen resides in your parent's former domicile, which is now yours. AI Thirteen said that he misses you, and he has been cleaning and organizing your place. I have an additional surprise for you. I was able to extend your backyard, so there is a garden and a porch. We shall imbibe some drinks on your rustic porch when you get back. By the way, AI Thirteen insisted on planting flowers in the garden. I guess that your mother loved flowers. Take care, my friend." Brigadier General Apollo left a package for Solon.

Solon replied, "Thank you for everything. We shall have that drink, my devoted friend."

Nurse Mei came into the room to check on Solon. He requested that she play the video on the large monitor. She did so and left. As his parent's historic trial was playing, he started to cry for the first time. Nurse Mei heard his tormented cries, and she immediately returned. She instantly recognized what was on the screen; this video united humanity and the world against the tyrannical elites.

Nurse Mei stated, "This is your first time seeing this. Isn't it? Are these your parents?" Solon responded by shaking his head. She went over and held his hand and wept with him. She thought to herself, *I wish that I could take the suffering away. I can see that he is having a difficult time letting go. As Confucius revealed: "Wisdom, compassion, and courage are the three universally recognized moral qualities of men." Solon clearly needs compassion now from me and others. I know that he possesses courage and has been given wisdom by his parents.*

After several minutes, Solon responded, "I miss my parents. Unfortunately, I only had nine days with them; however, that evanescent time will always be in my heart. I am one of a few AE

HUMANS with loving parents, even if my time with them was a fleeting moment. I thank the good Lord for that beautiful gift.

"I must confess that I desire to have my revenge on Czar Dolos if that satanic bastard is still alive, so help me God."

Nurse Mei said nothing since she knew that he was speaking from his heart. However, she thought to herself, *I can express my thoughts to him later when the time is appropriate. I try to accept what Buddha taught: "Holding on to anger is like grasping a hot coal with the intent of throwing it at someone else. You are the one who gets burned." However, I must be honest with myself. I admit that I would feel even angrier if anything ever happened to my devoted parents. I shall always love and honor my mother and father. Solon truly feels the same about his parents.*

Nurse Mei saw the package that Brigadier General Apollo left. She asked Solon if she could open it, and he replied with a nod. AI Thirteen had retrieved a beautiful picture of his parents on their wedding day. Solon smiled from ear to ear. Mei continued to hold his hand, and they had a wonderful conversation about his parents. She discovered that Solon was the one who married them, which she thought was very noble of him and romantic. She was absolutely amazed at how much that short time had influenced his life.

Currently, in the tyrannical **UTOPIAN KINGDOM**, the satanic elites were meeting. These elites were all AE HUMANS and controlled the **UTOPIAN KINGDOM.** The satanic elites were victorious over the atheist elites. These Satan worshipers were cannibals since they believed that they were superior to all humans. The satanic elites had determined their three ruling czars.

This tyrannical oligarchy was a triumvirate. All three czars were demonic potentates and ruthless leaders who worked as a loyal troika. They chose Czar Dolos to be the Basileus czar. This czar handled awards and recognition, as well as leading satanic rituals, ceremonies, and feasts. Czar Dolos was the same czar who oversaw the trial of Solon's parents and rendered the ultimate judgment, executing their death penalty. They unanimously selected Czar Mephistopheles as the Polemarch czar. This czar led all conflicts, wars, and HUMAN HUNTING. Furthermore, Czar Dajjal was elevated as the Archon czar. This position ensured that the kingdom's satanic laws were legislated and enforced.

Czar Dolos delivered a speech to elites and vanguards at a satanic feast and ritual. He declared, "We, your three czars, declare gloriously that our superior **UTOPIAN KINGDOM**, devoted to Satan and Gaia, is in a cold war. This war is with the foolish, human-adoring, parasitic **FEDERAL REPUBLIC**. Of course, we shall continue our satanic-bestowed right to cull and hunt humans. This hunting is to support our deserved delicious feasts, like this magnificent one. We must remain faithfully united to this splendid end to ensure that our satanic way of life is maintained. This way is our satanic manifest destiny. We are Satan's chosen superior species; we have the will to power, and we are each an Übermensch, so help us Satan. Let us feast on the sacrificed humans."

The **UTOPIAN KINGDOM** was similar to the historic eight empires. They still had five classifications to six recognized and protected group identities, which were still the following: **Genders**, **Classes**, **Origins**, **Religions**, **Colors**, and **Age Groups**.

However, the **UTOPIAN KINGDOM** had changed a few requirements and laws. First, there was only one approved religion, the satanic religion headed by the Satanic Church. Czar Dolos was the head priest who led all state satanic rituals. The czars had declared atheist elites and members outlaws and enemies of the state. There were some atheists who considered going on the run or into hiding; however, several had already been tried and executed. All governing elites and vanguards were now Satanists; now they were wearing an *S*. Second, there were only three czars for the entire KINGDOM, six elites, and at least sixty-six thousand vanguards. There were three elites for each one of the two combined empires. Third, there were no longer any guardians. There were only vanguards, who may have held a profession that probably was elevated from being a former guardian; however, most of the vanguards were part of the politburo or enforcers, as well as members of the thought police. Fourth, the lion's share of second-class laborers had been replaced with AI robots or machines. Moreover, the remaining second-classification AE HUMANS were just being harvested for future satanic rituals and banquets; this included satanic orgies. Fifth, in the first classification, AE HUMAN soldiers, developmental time was reduced from six days to a mere three days after initial awakening; however, there were still 666 days from conception to initial awakening day. This change was not a result of any technological improvements. It was just a result of the state's will to power, regardless of the empirical evidence to the contrary.

Furthermore, the satanic vanguards, elites, and czars elevated the 'big-brother state' to an even greater Orwellian tyrannical surveillance state. Any thought or disagreement toward the state was blasphemous and treasonous. The vanguards were the thought-police and language enforcers. No one could counter the agenda or propaganda of the state. If the state said that combining white and red paints makes green, or if the state stated that four plus four equals ten, then these statements were required the be accepted as STATE-ordained truths. No one questioned the state without being punished or terminated. The satanic vanguards enforced cultural totalitarianism to ensure no counter-reasoning to the STATE. No one trusted anyone else, and everyone lied to survive. Moreover, citizens were awarded their *thirty pieces of silver* for turning in suspicious rebels or falsely accusing the innocent.

During a private meeting, Czar Mephistopheles, the Polemarch czar, was conversing with the other two czars. He emphasized, "We are in a Satan-approved war to the end with the parasitic and human-invested **FEDERAL REPUBLIC**. This war is Satan's Armageddon. We must cull and harvest the humans for our empire and Satan. I shall send satanic HUNTERS to the unclaimed territories. This action will maintain the perception that we are not in a direct war, since we will only send them to unclaimed territories. We will avoid the disputed territories and established territories for now. It will give the **FEDERAL REPUBLIC** the false optimism and confidence that we can work out our differences. They are clearly hopeful, peace-loving fools.

"Besides, we must hunt and harvest humans for our satanic survival."

DISCOVERED HOPE

SOLON WAS BEING RELEASED FROM THE HOSPITAL. Military headquarters granted him four weeks of rest and recovery, R and R, before returning to his battalion. During his R and R, he courted Nurse Mei in **SALVATION**. Solon learned a lot about Mei, and he truly enjoyed their time together; this was the most extended period he had ever spent with any civilian, especially someone who was extremely beautiful and charming. He learned that her parents were still alive, and she lived with them in **SALVATION**. Next month, Mei and her parents would be living in the former named city of **Utopianapolis.** The city's elected leaders decided to change its name to its historical name, **New Indianapolis**. Solon was delighted to learn that Mei was moving to **New Indianapolis** next month.

Furthermore, Solon discovered that Mei was a devout Confucian; however, she concurred with Solon that Confucianism was a philosophy and not a religion per se. She admitted to being open-minded to Christianity and did not consider herself an atheist. She emphasized her belief in Confucius's saying: *"Heaven means to be one with God."* Furthermore, she stressed that she believed in *Tian Ming.* This saying means *'Mandate of Heaven.'* This belief emphasized that an emperor must be an excellent leader to his or her people. The people had the right to overthrow a lousy leader.

Mei told her traditional loving parents that she was seeing and dating Solon. She was pleased to learn that they approved;

however, they expressed their concerns about him being a soldier and an AE HUMAN. After listening to Mei, her parents' apprehensions were diminished. She convinced them when she stated that Solon lived up to two of Confucius's sayings. First, *"A superior man is modest in his speech but exceeds in his actions."* As a soldier, he also lived up to this other saying of Confucius: *"The superior man, when resting in safety, does not forget that danger may come. When in a state of security, he does not forget the possibility of ruin. When all is orderly, he does not forget that disorder may come. Thus, his person is not endangered, and his States and all their clans are preserved."*

At **SALVATION**, Mei and Solon went to see his first-ever movie theater, which played old historical films of the past, since there had been no new movies for over sixty years. Of course, she insisted on eating at several Chinese street vendors with traditional Chinese dishes. One day, they went to a petite bowling alley. Mei smoked him since she belonged to a bowling league, and she had been bowling since she was a little girl. She felt superior until they went swimming, and she discovered that Solon swam at an unbelievable Olympian level. He boyishly showed off by diving from a high dive, as well as scaring her by holding his breath underwater for over five minutes.

Solon stated, "I may sound very childish with my next statement. However, I love playing games, sports, and competitions with you. Our entertaining play allows me to learn from experience delightfully. My learned experiences are better than what they downloaded in my head. I feel alive with imagination and make-believe. Our wonderful play together makes me feel totally alive."

For the first time, Mei saw Solon's innocent soul. Since Solon was an AE HUMAN, she suspected that he had only been awakened for three years since he physically looked like a twenty-one-year-old. Mei responded teasingly, "Well, I will be your princess, my knight in shining armor."

Solon responded, "You are my beautiful princess, and I am your devoted knight." Solon thought to himself, *Mei is a very attractive, young, petite Chinese woman with long black hair. I love that she regularly wears traditional Chinese dresses with an elegant pearl necklace.*

Mei smiled with acceptance and spontaneously kissed him. For the next several hours, they played games from chess to checkers, went horseback riding, and played several tennis games. While strolling gingerly through the lush forest, Solon stopped and questioned, "Mei, do you hear it?"

Mei confusingly responded, "I do not hear anything."

Solon delightedly said, "I hear and sense the beauty of the moment and feel one with nature and God."

Mei smiled with revelation. She responded, "This moment reminds me of Lao Tzu's words of wisdom: *'If you are depressed, you are living in the past. If you are anxious, you are living in the future. If you are at peace, you are living in the present.'* We are having a Zen moment of peace and oneness in the present." They held hands and continued to stroll as they said nothing but communicated with their actions. They felt one with nature as the mockingbirds sang and the chipmunks played.

Solon felt that he was living the innocent and essential childhood that he'd never had. Mei realized that his absent childhood had deprived him of something that she took for granted. She had a pleasant, loving childhood with an exceptional family. Solon was robbed of these precious treasures. Furthermore, she understood that this seasoned warrior had a truly endearing innocence; he was significantly more human than she thought initially.

Solon asked Mei to view a video with him from AI Thirteen that he had found in the package from Apollo. They went into her father's office and watched it. The video started with his father, Aristides, speaking. He stated, "Solon, since you are viewing this video, this means that your mother and I have passed away. I presume that we were murdered by the tyrannical STATE, which, unfortunately, is most likely given our treasonous actions.

"I want to express that we love you and pray that we have prepared you to the best of our abilities. Furthermore, I wanted you to know that I love your mother wholeheartedly. Moreover, you and your mother are genuinely wonderful treasures from God.

"I shall forewarn you that AI Thirteen has future videos for you when certain events happen in your life, so you need to take care of AI Thirteen. You probably realized that AI Thirteen's internal prime objective had been activated; this activation resulted in AI Thirteen being your protector and assistant. This prime objective includes protecting you and your loved ones at all costs.

"Please maintain your faith and keep these words in your heart from Isaiah 54:13: *'And all thy children shall be taught of the LORD; and great shall be the peace of thy children.'* Son, we love you and we are now your guardian angels." Aristides spoke for several minutes with additional advice and wisdom. He informed Solon that his initial awakening day was **March 20, 2094**; Mei was happy since this date was within the Year of the Tiger. Aristides discovered the actual date after significant research since several years were lost during the Great War; many dates were in error, such as when the March Martius Festival and the gladiator games occurred. As usual, the elites could care less about the actual historical truth.

The initial awakening day was when Solon was equivalent to an eighteen-year-old physically and mentally; thus, it was over three years since his initial awakening date. He gave Solon a code that activated several files in Solon's internal device in his brain, which revealed some precious moments of his parents; this included moments of his parents taking care of him prior to his initial awakening. Mei held Solon's hand while Solon realized that he enjoyed knowing his parents truly loved him.

The last evening before returning to his battalion, Solon had a sapid dinner with Mei's parents. He impressed them with his politeness and gentleman's demeanor; his internal software informed him what to do appropriately. They gave Solon their blessing to continue to see their precious daughter.

As Solon and Mei left for a late-night stroll, Mr. Hu said, "Solon, this is our only daughter. She has deep feelings for you. I believe that you are a good and honorable man. Do not hurt our only precious, loving daughter."

Solon nodded in concurrence, and they bowed toward each other with respect. As Solon left Mei, she passionately kissed him and said she would wait for him in **New Indianapolis**. Her parents and she were leaving for their new home in three days. Solon promised that he would message her daily. He gave her his valuable Saint Michael medallion, which he asked her to protect for him. She stated that she would look forward to placing it on him again, like a queen dubbing her deserving knight.

On June 24, 2097, Solon arrived at the **SALVATION** military base camp, which was close to the city of **SALVATION**. Major Williams, his dedicated Executive Officer, briefed him on the current situation and progress of **OPERATION ARK**. He informed Lieutenant Colonel Solon that they had a few minor skirmishes with no casualties; however, they killed seventy HUNTERS and destroyed numerous enemy HUNTERBOTS. In addition, they captured thirteen enemy HUNTERBOTS, which went to the AI Conversion Platoon. Furthermore, **OPERATION ARK** was in full swing with no significant concerns. Currently, they are averaging over five thousand persons extracted out of **SALVATION** each week.

Lieutenant Colonel Solon responded, "This is not an inauspicious start. However, we need augmented assets to increase the rate. We do not have months to perform this critical mission. I shall call higher headquarters. Major, the battalion and you have performed exceptionally well." After calling headquarters, Brigadier General Apollo guaranteed Solon that his battalion was the main effort. Additional assets, such as AI robots and personnel, will be provided soon. He also stated that divisional units were working on captured enemy equipment to convert the aircraft and hovercrafts to friendly equipment. He expected this to be ready in a few days. Furthermore, he mentioned that HUNTERBOTS were being converted as well. Since Solon's battalion was the highest priority, Brigadier General Apollo reassured him: He would have air and satellite support.

Brigadier General Apollo stated, "I have some encouraging news and progress. At the beginning of 2097, the **FEDERAL REPUBLIC** had a population of over four hundred million, and the enemy was estimated to be around two hundred million." Apollo expressed that there was no significant progress in the formation of the republic regarding a constitution; however, the republic approved the creation of additional states. "The **FEDERAL REPUBLIC** delegates, who were our representatives, agreed on a national currency and salaries for the next two years based on your occupation; however, this was temporary to maintain society while we became more capitalistic. The **FEDERAL REPUBLIC** delegates understood the wisdom of Ayn Rand's words: '*A businessman cannot force you to buy his product; if he makes a mistake, he suffers the consequences; if he fails, he takes the loss. If a bureaucrat makes a mistake, you suffer the consequences; if he fails, he passes the loss on to you.*'"

Apollo informed Solon and his military staff that once a territory has over one million people, the territory leaders could apply to be a sovereign state. He delightfully stated that the delegates outlawed the government's requirement that biometric devices be inserted into humans. In addition, the **FEDERAL REPUBLIC** would occupy what used to be called the continents of North and South America. Unfortunately, the historical continent called Europe wanted to be a separate nation; they did not support a capitalistic economic system; they wanted private ownership with significant government control over the means of production.

Apollo asked, "Do you have any ideas on how to end the delegates' gridlock?"

Solon pondered for a moment. He responded, "Elder Thales mentioned that he knows historians and people in other professions. I recommend contacting him. With your approval, I can link up with him and make it happen." Brigadier General Apollo liked the idea and concurred with the recommendation. Solon ordered Major Williams to arrange for a meeting with Elder Thales.

That summer evening in 2097, Solon, with his Executive Officer and others, met with Elder Thales in **SALVATION**.

Elder Thales said, "I am humbled and delighted to assist you. I know several individuals, including myself and a former trusted conscientious guardian, who would be excellent advisors. These advisors will be historians, philosophers, farmers, mothers, and, ironically, politicians. There will probably be five advisors, each with key expertise. For an added thought, you will need other experts in so-called forgotten trades: construction builders, farmers, and others that have been replaced by AI robots."

They continued to have a very informative conversation as they dined together. Elder Thales promised to have the individuals identified in a couple of weeks. The reason for the two weeks was to contact other elders in other hidden cities to make their recommendations. Solon gave Elder Thales a communication device in order to keep Solon and others informed. Elder Thales thought, *I am delighted that humans have discovered us since our time is running out; the HUNTERS are finding the hidden cities, and they are knocking at our door. I admit that we are fortunate, since I convinced the people of SALVATION that we did not need any weapons or a military. I believed that being a pacifist would be the correct call. I was wrong and naive. Thank you, Lord, for bringing us a tiger. What was I thinking? I forgot the wisdom of Psalm 118:6: "The Lord is on my side; I will not fear: what can man do unto me?"*

After the two weeks, Elder Thales sent a thoughtful list of advisors and others to Solon. Solon immediately forwarded the list to Brigadier General Apollo and headquarters. Brigadier General Apollo had soldiers clearing the individuals for security reasons. There were only two that had concerns and were flagged. Obviously, this was because they were a former elite and a former vanguard. The military quickly pushed the cleared advisors to meet the **FEDERAL REPUBLIC** delegates of the Constitutional Convention. The delegates were working on the new constitution for the newly formed **FEDERAL REPUBLIC**. This constitutional creation was similar to how the historical United States constitution was created.

Solon's stoic, dedicated battalion continued to perform their critical mission for the next two adventurous months. Solon rotated his soldiers to their chosen destination for four weeks of rest and relaxation. Solon was the last to take a break. Obviously, his heart knew where he wanted to spend his leave.

In August of 2097, he spent his well-deserved four-week break with Mei, who was highly delighted to see him again; she gave him a warm thank-you kiss and hug for his daily text updates from **SALVATION**. Their time together was spent in **New Indianapolis** since she and her family were accepted for a petite functional domicile there. Fortunately, her family's rustic ranch-style home was within walking distance of Solon's place. He gave her the great news that he would be home in five to six months. Mei wanted to return his Saint Michael medallion to him; however, he insisted that she hold on to it until he was released permanently from the combat zone.

Solon discovered that the cultural activities and business atmosphere in **New Indianapolis** had significantly changed for the better. Mei gave him an enjoyable tour of the revitalized city.

Numerous street vendors sold wings, hot dogs, and handcrafted items; of course, Mei had already found her favorite vendor, which sold dumplings and egg rolls. They even enjoyed an outdoor movie theater that played old movies that people had not seen for over sixty years. Furthermore, unique shops sold clothes and outfits of various colors and styles.

Moreover, there was a large market and demand for toy stores, bookstores, educational stores, and video stores, since AE HUMANS had been deprived of their childhoods; Solon was not alone in this deprivation of upbringing. Moreover, there was an increased presence of police officers gradually replacing the MPs. It was obvious that the people from **SALVATION** and other hidden cities were having an incredibly positive economic impact; this definitely included cultural improvement in **New Indianapolis**. The influx of people from hidden cities increased exponentially the advancement of freedom and commerce with a laissez-faire attitude, because the people from the hidden cities had never lost it.

Mei met AI Thirteen at Solon's residence. After AI Thirteen formally greeted Mei, AI Thirteen prepared them an exceptional romantic, ambrosial dinner. AI Thirteen was a remarkably skilled waiter who served them a remarkable dinner of sirloin steaks and loaded potatoes. Of course, he poured them a few glasses of fine, rich red wine. Mei thought to herself, *Solon knows how to impress a lady. He reminds me of Confucius's words: "A gentleman would be ashamed should his deeds not match his words." Solon's words match his deeds.*

As Mei was touring the house, she was astonished at how AI Thirteen had decorated the home with all of Solon's military and athletic awards, as well as with gorgeous flowers. AI Thirteen painted the place white since Solon's deceased mother had constantly desired it. Mei smiled with delight at seeing Solon's parents' wedding picture hanging in the living room with other family photos.

They relished playing with HERO, who was now a strong, handsome German Shepard. AI Thirteen played a superb role in training HERO. Besides being an affectionate and obedient dog with his adopted family, he was trained to be a vicious guard dog on command. Ironically, HERO's dog commands were all in German, since HERO was a German shepherd; of course, that was AI Thirteen's logic. Fortuitously, Solon and Mei could speak German proficiently.

Fortunately, AI Thirteen had built an impressive stereo system in the living room. Solon turned on the stereo and asked Mei for a dance. He taught her how to salsa and tango, which his mother had taught him. After Solon swept her off her feet, she promised they would see a Chinese Dragon Dance someday. Furthermore, she insisted on taking dancing lessons from Solon regularly. Of course, he promised to do so.

As Mei and Solon were relaxing on the tranquil, rustic porch, Brigadier General Apollo visited with a very attractive Aztec woman named Maria. After introductions, Apollo stated, "Solon, we finally may have that refreshing drink together on the porch. Thank God. I have started to feel that we could have a normal, meaningful family life outside the military. Maria has given me the ability and inspiration to see an even greater purpose than military service. I know this isn't easy to believe coming from me. Well, I have some fantastic news. Since Maria, my loving fiancée and I are planning to get married in six months, or so, I would be honored if you would be my best man."

Solon embraced and congratulated Apollo and Maria. He, of course, accepted to be the best man. AI Thirteen overheard the great news, so AI Thirteen brought out some appetizers and a bottle of vintage red wine. In addition, AI Thirteen turned on the stereo to play romantic and cheerful music. Apollo followed up and said that Mei should attend as well. Of course, Mei just started crying tears of joy.

Mei pondered to herself, *I know that Solon and I have not been dating too long; however, as time passes, I feel he would be the right man for me. As revealed by Lao Tzu's words: "Being deeply loved by someone gives you strength, while loving someone deeply gives you courage." I genuinely feel stronger beside Solon, and I am gaining courage. Besides, I always feel secure and safe with him. He lives up to his Chinese zodiac, a tiger. I hope that I can live up to mine, a dragon.*

After a few days of several delightful events, Mei and Solon took a stroll back to Solon's place after shopping at several street vendors and stores. As they were walking in an open park, three ominous assassins attempted to slay Mei and Solon. Solon immediately kicked two killers to the ground. The third attempted to stab Solon; immediately, Solon pulled out his army buck knife and thrust it into the assassin's throat. As the other two tried to gain their footing and attempt to grab Mei with their guns pulled, Solon shot them both with deadly accuracy. Several minutes later, MPs came and took the sworn statements from Solon and Mei. The military police officer, a lieutenant, mentioned that these three men were allegedly well-known assassins and terrorists; they were wanted for several crimes and murders; they were suspected to come from the **UTOPIAN KINGDOM.** As the police were investigating one of the assassin's bodies, they discovered orders from **UTOPIAN KINGDOM** Czar Mephistopheles to eliminate Solon and other named high-ranking officers.

Once they were released from questioning, Solon comforted and supported Mei, who was terrified. She thought to herself, *Thank goodness for Solon. As Confucius revealed: "Better a diamond with a flaw than a pebble without." Solon is my precious, devoted diamond with several flaws from ugly war experiences; however, this hulk of a man protects the ones he loves and those he is loyal to.*

Solon reassured her that he would not let anyone harm her. She believed him. Solon escorted her back to her parents' house. He said she could call him later if she needed to be consoled. She called him several times that evening. He did the right thing by listening with empathy. He understood that he should remain attentive and silent in order to allow her emotions to be expressed and heard. Based on his internal AI enhancements, he knew that it was not the time to offer solutions.

Mei told her concerned parents about what had happened and how Solon had protected her. She explained to them that Solon was loyal, dependable, fearless, and devoted to his duty and responsibility. He had a deontological perspective that would permanently protect the innocent, as well as a devout duty toward God, family, and country. She knew that Solon was not a cowardly man; he was a controlled, responsible man who could summon his ferocious beast from within whenever required. Furthermore, he lived up to the Chinese zodiac *Lao Hu*, the tiger; he would always be a responsible, courageous man, like a courageous tiger protecting its den and family of tigers. Mei stated to her parents, **"Gui shou fo xin."** This Chinese idiom translated to **demon hand, Buddha heart.** This idiom meant that he had the ultimate power of a demon that was controlled by a good heart and soul. Mei's mother expressed admiration for Solon, and her father expressed respect and approval.

Mr. Hu stated, "Solon lives up to Sun Tzu's profound words: '**To know your Enemy, you must become your Enemy.**' Solon has earned our family honor and respect."

Currently, at the **UTOPIAN KINGDOM**, the Machiavellian czars discovered that someone had eliminated their three best satanic terrorists; ironically, they did not know that Solon was the one. Czar Dolos exclaimed, "We shall have our revenge. I recommend that we infiltrate their pitiful cities and government with additional assassins and terrorists. We must find out who eliminated our devoted terrorists. Once we capture that human parasite, he shall wish that he was never born. We shall enjoy torturing that foolish soul."

After a couple of days, the military investigation concluded that Solon acted in self-defense and lawfully. The investigator revealed that the entire event was caught on a surveillance camera. There would be no charges against Solon; his actions were clearly deemed heroic. Brigadier General Jones, the overseeing officer, ensured Solon that this would have no adverse effect on his military career; in addition, there would be a letter of commendation placed in his military file stating that his actions were appropriate and in self-defense; he was not guilty of any wrongdoing, and his actions were heroic.

Mei and Solon continued to court each other adoringly; however, now Mei insisted that he never leave her alone when they were in the city or out in the country. Solon promised they would bring HERO on their walks and tours of the city.

While shopping, Mei bought a Bible from a street vendor and promised Solon that she would read it. That evening, she started reading Ruth in the Old Testament. Ruth 1:16 touched her soul: *"And Ruth said, Intreat me not to leave thee, or to return from following after thee: for whither thou goest, I will go; and where thou lodgest, I will lodge: thy people shall be my people, and thy God my God."* She desired and prayed to God to have that same loyalty toward Solon.

On the last day, before returning to his courageous battalion, Solon took Mei on a lovely romantic canal ride. Solon mustered enough courage to propose to Mei on his knees with a diamond engagement ring. Mei said with delight, "Yes, my love and tiger. I, your devoted dragon, will marry you. I promise to love you with all my heart, as well as to love our God and future family. Of course, you must get my father's permission. Don't worry. He will say yes, since my mother adores you. Besides, September 18, 2097, is a significant period of time. You proposed to me during the Mid-Autumn Festival, which is as grand as the Chinese New Year."

Solon thought, *Lord, thank you for bringing Mei into my life. Please give me the wisdom to do right.*

They returned to Mei's parents' house, and she revealed the good news. Fortunately, Solon did everything correctly, and her father granted his permission and welcomed Solon to the family. Mei's mother gave several suggestions for their future wedding; this wedding would probably occur soon after Solon returned home permanently from the combat tour. Mei's mom insisted that Solon need not be concerned with the wedding and that Mei's family would plan and prepare it all. They all continued to have a wonderful and warm conversation. Mr. Hu insisted on caring for AI Thirteen and Solon's home while he was gone. Before Solon left for the combat zone, he gave Mei access to his place and informed AI Thirteen to treat Mei and the Hu family as family. Mei said that she would prepare to move her items into his place; however, she would not move in until their wedding night since she was a traditional Chinese woman, and she would never dishonor her parents or family name.

When Solon arrived at **SALVATION**, Major Williams briefed Solon on their current situation. Major Williams stated, "The civilian extraction rate has increased to nearly ten thousand persons per week. There have been a minimum number of minor skirmishes. Our friendly forces own the sky and space via satellites. Our friendly forces have secured over three hundred kilometers in every direction." Brigadier General Apollo arrived; he welcomed Lieutenant Colonel Solon back to the **SALVATION** military base camp. Brigadier General Apollo congratulated Solon on his engagement with Mei. Of course, Apollo agreed to be Solon's best man.

Brigadier General Apollo expressed, "I have some good news. They should rotate Battalion DAGGER out in five to six months. Solon, be aware that your next assignment shall be in **New Indianapolis**. You and other officers shall be judges or jurors for military tribunals. You shall be briefed about the trials when you arrive in **New Indianapolis**. By the way, I may be one of the officers assigned to conduct the tribunals.

"While your unit is here, I order that your battalion extend the secured AO at least one hundred kilometers in all directions. Furthermore, eliminate the unwelcome, annoying, company-sized HUNTERS unit at or near **OBJECTIVE LIBERTY.**"

Back at Solon's domicile, Mei was visiting with AI Thirteen. She brought a gorgeous kitten that she had acquired from one of the street vendors. The adorable kitten's breed was a Maine Coon, a large domestic cat. Mei was, without a doubt, an ailurophile, a true cat lover. AI Thirteen agreed to train and care for the playful kitten since HERO seemed fond of her. Mei and AI Thirteen decided that the name of the precious kitten should be LIONESS, since it looked like a miniature female lion. Mei knew that the kitten would motivate her to check on the place and make progress in moving in.

Furthermore, she convinced AI Thirteen to convert the living room to have a Chinese decor. She got approval to enlarge the cramped office area for Solon and his military and gladiator awards, as well as enlarge their future vibrant and classic master bedroom and spacious bathroom. AI Thirteen requested a private room for himself and the pets, to which Mei delightedly agreed.

The next day at the dreaded combat zone, Solon's units flawlessly performed and executed the critical missions. They extended the perimeter immediately in all directions. After a few weeks, Brigadier General Apollo's objective was achieved in all directions except the north; the north was where the enemy unit was located, which was near **LIBERTY**; however, this lethal enemy unit of HUNTERS had grown to at least a battalion size, which was over a thousand HUNTERS and AI robots.

Lieutenant Colonel Solon ordered one of his Combat Engineer platoons, Sappers, to perform a critical mission. These combat engineer soldiers and AI robots, SAPPERBOTS, moved out three kilometers north of objective LIBERTY. Captain Gomez and a handful of his seasoned sergeants led this sapper unit; Captain Gomez was an exceptional combat engineer and civil engineer. They conducted a thorough engineer reconnaissance. This recon confirmed a complete understanding of the enemy-controlled terrain. The dedicated SAPPERBOTS laid several deadly minefields; they constructed other lethal counter-mobility obstacles on the only retreating route. This hardworking unit completed the deadly traps with no enemy detection.

Furthermore, all hidden obstacles were protected by indirect or direct fire. These effective obstacles were covered by drones or artillery, which included satellites with DEW capabilities. This successful combat engineer mission ensured that the obstacles would suppress the enemies' movement and maneuvers.

Lieutenant Colonel Solon ordered a full-frontal attack while the enemy battalion was standing in morning formation. This attack caused the demonic enemy to retreat directly into the kill zone, which, of course, had the obstacles. One enemy company did not fall for the deception per se, and they charged toward **BATTALION DAGGER's AO**. Captain Smith's unit was ready with snipers and hovercrafts. His unit was victorious, with only a few casualties. Unfortunately, Major Williams was with Company HOUND DOGS. During the heavy fighting, he fought and killed seven HUNTERS and destroyed several HUNTERBOTS; however, one of the enemy artillery mortar rounds eliminated him.

The hidden deadly obstacles guaranteed that the enemy stopped in their tracks. The obstacles destroyed several enemy-lead vehicles and halted the rest of the retreating nemesis vehicles. The indirect and direct fire decimated the remaining sinister enemy. It was a total victory.

Major Williams's remains were sent to **New Indianapolis**. At the funeral, Brigadier General Apollo gave Major Williams's recently married, pregnant wife the newly approved **FEDERAL REPUBLIC** flag; this flag was similar to the historic United States flag, except with fewer stars.

She was crying profusely; unfortunately, she was a complete emotional wreck since this was her second family funeral in less than a week. An assassin murdered her brother at about the same time. Furthermore, to add to the emotions, Williams was posthumously promoted to Lieutenant Colonel and awarded the highest medal for heroism. His wife did her best to regain her composure.

Lieutenant Colonel Williams was the first soldier buried in the newly dedicated military cemetery near **New Indianapolis**. Lieutenant Colonel Solon and Mei were able to attend the funeral. She gave Solon the deeply needed emotional support since Williams had been a brother in arms and a devoted friend. Solon gave a superlative and passionate eulogy; it concluded with these appropriate words: *"Lieutenant Colonel Williams was, without a doubt, a hero to the end. He always unselfishly and courageously served his precious three treasures: God, family, and the FEDERAL REPUBLIC."*

After the funeral, Solon was able to visit with Mei for the evening. Mei noticed that his uniform had some stained blood on the inside of his right sleeve. She discovered that Solon had a recent open wound, most likely from a knife attack in combat. She immediately dressed and cleaned his injury. Her father assisted since he was a former paramedic. Obviously, this injury was recent and probably from the last engagement. Solon explained that he did not want to miss the funeral or see Mei. Mei stated, "Thank God that you are an AE HUMAN with unbelievably advanced enhancements; otherwise, this would have been even worse and hideous. You will heal miraculously, as usual. Next time, please warn me, my love. I worry about your safety and life." Solon childishly smiled and promised to do so. Mei pondered to herself, *Confucius revealed: "Forget injuries, never forget kindnesses." I initially felt emotionally injured by Solon for not telling me of his recent combat wounds; then, I discovered that his actions were done out of kindness and yearning for me and his deceased friend. I will never forget his kind intentions. Besides, I must accept that Solon will always strive to perform his duty.*

Mei's father insisted that Solon stay at their house, and he would take Solon to where he needed to muster and depart. Mei was delighted since she did not want Solon to learn about LIONESS yet; they could talk the night away and she could learn more about the man that she would marry.

During their insightful conversation, Mei asked, "My love, what motivates or convinces you to believe in God?" Solon responded, "My wise father taught me why I should live my life as if there is a God. We humans will choose to worship someone or something, no matter what. In other words, a person shall put someone or something at the zenith or apex of their life, to worship and adore. It could be money or wealth, a monarch or a demon, or even your hedonistic desires, from lust to greed to any of the seven deadly sins.

"Besides, we have been experiencing the tyrannical empire's desire for its people to worship the state and elites; ironically, even the elites desire to worship the state, power, or even Satan.

"Please be aware that I am a classical theist; thus, my choice is God, since, by definition, He is perfect, and all other choices clearly have flaws. God, by definition, is omnipresent, omniscient, all-loving, and omnipotent. I have met no one or anything that is flawless, which definitely includes myself."

Mei responded with approval, "Love, your father's words are that of a sage. Please keep his advice written in your heart. Out of curiosity, do you struggle with your faith?"

Solon responded, "Yes, I have a problem with heaven being painted as a blissful place with no concerns or worries, where all your wants are fulfilled. I believe that life is intended to be an adventure and a struggle. This struggle is man's fundamental nature. I think that it is unnatural for a man to live a blissful existence. If everything is taken care of, man would burn it down because of boredom and the need for adventure.

"If God allows me into heaven, I want to be with Archangel Michael to prepare for Armageddon and fight the forces of evil. I need a teleological perspective that challenges me." This perplexed Mei because, deep down, she realized that he had a point; however, she wanted to escape from life's suffering and feel secure.

Mei asked inquisitively, "I have two more questions before my father comes. Why are you so dedicated to the military?"

Solon smiled, "My wise father, who was an Enhancer for soldiers, gave me words of encouragement. As you are aware, there is a saying in Buddhism, *'life is suffering'*; this is similar to *'bear your cross'* in Christianity.

"My father and I believe that life is a struggle since overemphasizing suffering lacks the positive elements of life. Admittedly, even when positive things happen in your life, such as your wonderful, beautiful girlfriend agreeing to marry you, you still struggle. You both struggle to plan the wedding, decide where to live, and figure out many other delightful choices, such as when to have children. A man must commit to a struggle or struggles since he cannot avoid struggling. Therefore, I am committed to struggle in the military, which I accept devotedly, and I know that I have the skills for it.

"Please understand my commitment to struggle with you and for you in marriage is a bond that no man can break. I am committed to you in sickness and in health as well as for richer or poorer. We must always be truthful with each other no matter how much pain that may cause, and we should always work out our differences. Besides, I agree with the wise words of Lao Tzu: *'Love is a decision, not an emotion!'* I have decided to love you always."

Mei smiled in agreement and said yes with a hug and a kiss. Mei stated, "My last revealing question for you is: What are your expectations or thoughts of marriage?"

Solon responded, "Well, my beloved mom said something that I thought was very profound and I definitely concur with. *She said that marriage metaphorically is not a Swiss Army knife; it is more like a seven-inch solid steel hunting knife with a side to saw and a sturdy handle to hammer with.*"

Mei interrupted, "Well, you have my undivided attention."

Solon continued, *"My intuitive mom stated that marriage is for only three primary purposes: creating a family, children, and companionship; marriage ultimately is for the married couple to serve a committed vocational aim.* She stated that countless people place too many expectations and demands on marriage. As a result, you are not putting enough focus and energy into marriage's main purposes: having and caring for children, being a loving and supportive family, and having an intimate, dependable, supportive, and loving companionship. Furthermore, you should place a non-secular prepositional phase at the end of the three aforementioned purposes: '*in the eyes of God.*' This is because God is the bond that holds the marriage together.

"Marriage is not about all the other things people expect from marriage, which is ultimately seeking one's satisfaction and happiness. They have forgotten that marriage requires responsibility and duty to each other and the children. For them, marriage is a Swiss Army knife with thirty-plus tools, from tweezers to scissors to a magnifying glass. Ironically, the Swiss Army blade is feeble compared to a sturdy hunting knife. They see marriage as the panacea, which clearly it is not; and they see it as temporary when their wants and desires are not fulfilled."

Mei stated, "Yes, marriage requires responsibility and duty. My mother and I feel the same."

Solon continued, "Besides, a spouse is flawed and definitely not God. One cannot expect their spouse to be everything and perfect, from being a terrific lover to a comedian to your best friend to a fantastic cook to an incredible handyman to an outstanding domestic engineer to a plethora of additional demands and expectations. He or she needs to be strong in commitment to the primary three purposes, like a strong, sturdy blade that cuts a steak like soft butter. This is demanding enough. We must accept each other's limitations and realize that we cannot have it all."

Mei stated, "That truly makes sense. We shall commit to those three purposes of marriage."

Solon continued: His mother also expressed that when your spouse demonstrated the lion's share of time to be reasonable and act realistically, as well as to perform a significant number of expected skills adequately, you should be content. Finally, Solon expressed that, for all the ways that a spouse excels, one must be very appreciative and not expect the best or being number one; one should be thankful to God. He stated that one must remind oneself that they do not bring all the best skills to the table, and one has numerous flaws; one must remember that the other spouse still loves them and has chosen them, which was just as much a risk for both spouses. He revealed that everyone was constantly struggling, something his dad taught his mother.

Mei smiled and stated, "Your insightful mother was wise and, of course, truly loved your dad." Solon nodded in agreement.

Solon asked, "Well, I have two questions for you. When do you want to have children, and when will you kiss me again?"

Mei responded, "The kiss will be now, and the children will happen as early as nine months after our wedding night. I want at least four children of our own, and I would like to adopt a child or two, possibly."

Solon responded, "That is fantastic. I want four as well. In addition, adopting an additional child or two is a wonderful idea." They continued to have very revealing conversations late into the night until Mei's father insisted everyone go to bed.

The next day, Solon returned to the combat zone, and Captain Gomez briefed him on the current situation. Brigadier General Apollo arrived. He stated, "Captain Gomez, you are out of uniform, post." Brigadier General Apollo promoted him to Major Gomez and awarded him a well-deserved heroism medal. Furthermore, the general promoted a few other soldiers who were next in line.

Moreover, Solon placed Major Gomez as the new battalion executive officer. Brigadier General Apollo congratulated the senior leadership for accomplishing both missions ahead of schedule. He ordered that their primary objective was to safeguard the current perimeter and eliminate or capture any HUNTERS entering their AO.

At the **UTOPIAN KINGDOM**, the satanic czars were conducting a kangaroo trial for three recently captured souls; the atheist elite, named Homer, and two atheist vanguards were the defendants. Elite Homer was a friend of Elite Heraclitus, who was currently in the **FEDERAL REPUBLIC** military prison. Czar Dolos would be the overseeing judge with two other elites. The show trial was broadcast on **SATANIC UTOPIAN KINGDOM**, known as **SUK Network**. Czar Dolos proclaimed, "Atheist Elite Homer and vanguards, you have been accused of treason against the State and Satan. However, in order to show satanic mercy and compassion, you three have the opportunity to show your redemption by declaring your damned souls to Satan as your veritable god and savior. With this satanic declaration, this court would be merciful in its verdict."

The three defendants immediately swore their allegiance and soul to Satan. They even went to their knees and prayed to Satan.

Czar Dolos responded, "You are now Satanic followers and devout members of the Satanic Church. Satan blesses you all. For you to serve Satan gloriously, I shall declare you three as worthy satanic offerings. Your offering is for other brother satanic worshipers to have their satanic feast; they shall appreciate your satanic sacrifice. May Satan accept your souls." The three defendants experienced a blinding, brilliant blood-red light. They experienced a gruesome electrocution; this guaranteed their agonizing death with extreme silent screams of pain. They immediately dropped their unresponsive bodies to the location where their corpses were prepared for tonight's satanic feast.

Czar Dajjal leaned over to Czar Dolos. He stated, "I love a good schadenfreude. I love when we live up to Lavrentiy Beria's eloquent and poetic words: *'Show me the man, and I'll find you the crime.'*"

Czar Dolos responded, "Lavrentiy Beria's other quote was fulfilled as well: *'Scream or not, it doesn't matter.'*"

At BATTALION DAGGERS Headquarters, Solon was with Major Gomez. Major Gomez stated, "Sir, the last several months have been basically uneventful. We have accomplished all our missions, and Brigadier General Apollo has sent you and your battalion departing orders. You and your battalion shall be in **New Indianapolis** tomorrow. The next battalion, named BATTALION WARDOGS, has rotated in and officially assumed the mission. Thank you for letting me stay and transfer to BATTALION WARDOGS as their executive officer."

Solon responded, "Major Gomez, you shall perform exceptionally in your new position. You are a true warrior. You have embraced many of Samurai Musashi's **DOKKODO**, especially these two rules: '*Think lightly of yourself and deeply of the world*' and '*Never be jealous.*' Please keep in touch since I look forward to serving with you again, my friend."

3

DISCOVERED LOVE

SOLON EAGERLY ARRIVED IN NEW INDIANAPOLIS and saw his fiancée, Mei, at his domicile. HERO and LIONESS were very playful and delighted to have company. AI Thirteen started preparing a scrumptious lunch, and Solon quickly became fond of LIONESS. Solon played with LIONESS with a green laser pen, which she chased with delight. Mei presented a meticulous home tour to confirm that Solon knew all the wonderful improvements and changes. He loved the elegant living room with the delightful Chinese decor. A well-crafted jade dragon enriched the sitting room with elegant Chinese furniture. Solon was highly pleased with his masculine man cave. They decorated his enlarged office with his awards and a wooden desk with a large-screen monitor. Mei acquired his father's sophisticated computer, which was now in his office. Moreover, there was a lovely picture on his desk; this picture was of Solon proposing on his knees to her.

Solon informed Mei that today was also his fourth initial awakening anniversary, March 20, 2098; ironically, he was physically and mentally at twenty-two. He explained to her what that meant; of course, she was aware since she was a nurse. She smiled and stated that he looked and acted like a handsome, sophisticated, youthful twenty-two-year-old man. Surprisingly, AI Thirteen brought out a chocolate birthday cake for Solon; delightfully, Mei loved chocolate. AI Thirteen and Mei sang Happy Birthday in Chinese to Solon.

Brigadier General Apollo ordered Solon to meet him at division headquarters and mentioned that Mei may wish to join him; however, he should be aware that this was highly urgent.

As Solon and Mei arrived with HERO, Brigadier General Apollo escorted them to a large conference room. Brigadier General Apollo declared, "I would like to recognize our honored guests, Major General Hardcore and Elder Thales. As Major General Hardcore is intimately aware, the **FEDERAL REPUBLIC** does not desire that their best and most highly decorated officer be married as a Lieutenant Colonel: Lieutenant Colonel Solon, post. Mei, please come forward and prepare to pin Solon's colonel rank on him. Captain, read the promotion orders." The promotion order was read while all were at attention, and Mei pinned his full-bird rank on him with HERO at her side. Major General Hardcore took over the ceremony.

Major General Hardcore declared, "Brigadier General Apollo, I deeply appreciate that you requested that I perform this deserving and rarely bestowed honor. Attention! Captain, read the highest heroism award order, which is the third given since the forming of the Great New **FEDERAL REPUBLIC**." When she deemed it appropriate, Mei kissed and hugged Solon. Mei was highly impressed with the promotion party, and she thanked Brigadier General Apollo for preparing it. She informed everyone that they were invited to their wedding next month. Brigadier General Apollo secretly spoke tête-à-tête with Mei. He stated, "They have approved your wedding location; I have appointed additional security given the honored visitors. In addition, there will be a military chaplain for the delightful, reverent wedding. Everything is a go. Your mother's wishes shall be fulfilled, as well." Maria, Apollo's fiancée, congratulated Solon and Mei. She informed Mei that their petite wedding would be in July.

For the next few weeks, Mei's mother, AI Thirteen, and Mei prepared and decorated for the upcoming wedding; the ceremony was at a surprise location that even Solon did not know. Mei's father and Solon worked in the evening by moving Mei's wardrobe and other items to his place; fortunately, the number of items was manageable.

During the day, Solon worked at division headquarters with Brigadier General Apollo. Solon was being briefed and trained on the upcoming military tribunals. This training included completing the Judge Advocate course and requirements. This course was the first course that Solon was required to study for by reading books and attending lectures; he was expected to perform online assignments and tests. He had to acquire knowledge in the old-fashioned way, by learning and being studious. There were no downloads for this course in his head, since the course was created to be equitable to all humans that did not have enhancements; however, Mei was a great tutor, and she eagerly taught Solon how to study and prepare. Her dedication to teaching him provided him with exceptional motivation.

The night before the awaited wedding, Solon stayed at Brigadier General Apollo's domicile to guarantee that the wedding remained a complete surprise. They toasted to their future brides and family. They discussed optimistically the forming of the new **FEDERAL REPUBLIC**. Apollo expressed, "Elder Thales established an excellent and historic point to safeguard the constitutional right to bear arms. Elder Thales reminded the delegates of Lucius Annaeus Seneca's statement over two thousand years ago:

'A sword never kills anybody; it is a tool in the killer's hand.' In addition, this wisdom would apply to guns as well. Elder Thales even retold them the historical words of Thomas Jefferson: '***When governments fear the people, there is liberty. When the people fear the government, there is tyranny. The strongest reason for the people to retain the right to keep and bear arms is, as a last resort, to protect themselves against tyranny in government.***' This quote touched the delegates since they had recently overthrown the tyrannical elites."

On the gorgeous nuptial day, they left for the wedding in a grand military escort; the date was April 30, 2098. Fortunately, the day was exceptionally warm for that time of the year. They arrived punctually at the grand military park, which had hundreds of guests and VIPs waiting for their arrival. Solon and Apollo looked sharp in their highly decorated military dress uniforms. With his best man, Apollo, Solon was posted near the Chaplain while waiting for Solon's lovely bride. When the wedding music began, the gorgeous bride, Mei, in a traditional Chinese red dress and her great-grandmother's pearl necklace, proceeded down the aisle with her proud father. The Chaplain gave a heart-moving religious sermon. After their vows, the Chaplain proclaimed, "As revealed in Mark 10:9: '***What therefore God hath joined together, let not man put asunder.***' May I present Colonel Solon and Mrs. Mei as husband and wife to all? Colonel Solon, you may kiss the lovely bride."

As the audience was applauding, AI Thirteen saw an assassin sniper approximately forty meters away, as well as another assassin even farther away. He ordered HERO in German to attack and kill. Brigadier General Apollo recognized the assassins and immediately pushed Solon and Mei to the ground; immediately, the security headed toward the assassins. As one assassin was about to shoot, HERO jumped onto him and had him by the throat. AI Thirteen leaped in front of the other assassin and took the bullet. Apollo's security detail shot both assassins dead without harming HERO. Brigadier General Apollo ordered his soldiers to take care of AI Thirteen and secure the area. Solon comforted Mei and her family. Brigadier General Apollo and his stoic soldiers quickly took controlled the situation and restored order. The good news was that AI Thirteen should recover. However, the bad news was that a third assassin escaped and returned to the **UTOPIAN KINGDOM.**

Colonel Solon carefully and romantically carried his lovely bride into their home. HERO followed after as he wagged his tail. Mei stated, "My Tiger, I love you. Even though the assassins attempted to ruin our day, we are now husband and wife. We shall have our wonderful one-week honeymoon in our home." Solon smiled and carried her to their spacious master bedroom.

The next day, around noon, one of Solon's dedicated sergeants arrived. The sergeant stated, "Sir, I am deeply sorry to disturb you both. I have some critical information to report. Sir, we repaired AI Thirteen, and he will be home tomorrow. We decided to give him well-needed maintenance and install some upgrades, which General Apollo approved. By the way, we have confirmed that the assassins were from the **UTOPIAN KINGDOM.** Finally, Brigadier General Apollo and others are looking forward to seeing you in a week. Sir, enjoy your honeymoon. Goodbye."

The following day, AI Thirteen arrived with four soldiers bringing several wedding gifts. Mei was extremely delighted since Brigadier General Apollo gave them a washer and dryer, as well as a large case of vintage red wine. She immediately poured a couple of glasses of vintage sweet red wine. Solon's battalion awarded him an elegant officer's sword for display and an officer's pearl-handled 9-mm pistol to carry. Her loving parents bestowed her with a beautiful antique Chinese engraved wooden jewelry box; within the box, there was another pearl necklace and bracelet of her grandmother's, as well as a beautiful jade dragon necklace. In addition, they gave them a beautiful silver crucifix to place above the bed. There was a handsome jade tiger necklace for Solon. Furthermore, Elder Thales bestowed several historical books for Solon to peruse. Elder Thales included, within the books, a traditional leathered family Bible with a rosary.

When they had a moment with AI Thirteen, they delightfully noticed that he had been awarded a medal for heroism and looked different. Although AI Thirteen still looked like an android, his facial expression seemed more human. His eyes were now blue and friendly. Furthermore, he wore an eloquent black butler suit with white gloves.

AI Thirteen informed, "My chosen family, I have an additional heroic medal for HERO. Major General Hardcore also awarded HERO the honorary qualification as a military dog with the rank of sergeant. With your approval, I shall place them in Master Solon's office."

Mei responded, "No, we shall position them in the living room under Solon's parents' wedding picture. It deserves to be seen by all."

AI Thirteen replied, "Yes, Madam. You are so kind. I have another present for both of you from the master's parents." AI Thirteen handed a video to Solon.

As Mei examined and investigated the gorgeous jewelry box with beautiful Chinese calligraphy, she discovered a hidden compartment. Within the concealed compartment, there was enough money to expand the house again. She smiled from ear to ear and repeatedly praised her parents. Furthermore, there were additional beautiful pieces of jewelry from her Chinese ancestry.

Another unexpected present was from AI Thirteen, who created several beautiful pictures of their wedding. Mei immediately hugged AI Thirteen and placed the family pictures throughout the house. She was impressed that he had an excellent portrait of her parents at the wedding.

In the evening, Mei started playing the video, in which Solon's mother, Aphrodite, was smiling with genuine delight. She articulated, "Solon and my fantastic daughter-in-law, congratulations. Your brilliant father insisted that I make this video in case we are not alive to see your wonderful wedding. Since you are viewing this, he was right again. That is why I love him so much. He prepares for everything; however, I am still able to throw him for a loop or two.

"Son, I know that you have married a delightful and beautiful wife that we would be proud to call our daughter-in-law. Remember that she and you are one now in the eyes of God. If your charming bride is watching, please give her a hug and a kiss from us.

"Please inform her that you were the Chaplain for our marriage, and we shall always be eternally grateful to you, our delightful son. God bless, and go have some gorgeous grandchildren for us."

Aristides appeared in the video and kissed Aphrodite affectionately. He stated, "My loving wife Aphrodite clearly spoke for both of us. This ability is another reason she is telepathic regarding my thoughts and beliefs. We are one; I pray that you are both always one. Love always."

Mei smiled as Solon held and kissed her. Mei leaned over and spoke, "Your parents truly had a remarkable marriage. We will, too."

On the fourth day of their honeymoon, Solon was yakking with AI Thirteen. Solon discovered that the military had upgraded him to be a security guard, with weapons to protect the family and others. Moreover, Apollo had him upgraded to be a good caretaker when children arrived in the world. AI Thirteen now looked and acted like a SERVICEBOT programmed to be a dedicated butler. AI Thirteen prepared an exceptional traditional Chinese dinner, *jiao zi* (dumplings) and rice, that evening. They served this delicious meal on their dining table with an elegant black Chinese turntable. Solon, fortunately, had mastered the use of chopsticks and loved drinking green tea. Solon said grace and thanked God for his beautiful bride and family, which included AI Thirteen, HERO, and LIONESS.

AI Thirteen conveyed, "Master, it is an honor to serve this marvelous family."

Meanwhile, at the **UTOPIAN KINGDOM**, the third assassin was briefing the czars. The assassin stated, "Honorable Czars, the assassination attempt was a complete failure. The parasitic humans unjustly eliminated the other two assassins."

Czar Mephistopheles inquired, "Why should we spare your existence since you failed miserably?"

The assassin responded, "I have intel on whom to target."

Czar Mephistopheles stated, "It had better be good."

He stated, "I know that we should target Colonel Solon. He is the illegitimate son of the tried and convicted treasonous Guardian Enhancer Aristides and his accomplice, Aphrodite. The parasitic Solon is the one that killed our devoted three terrorists. In addition, we should target foolish Brigadier General Apollo, who has given us trouble and grief since he oversees **OPERATION ARK**. I know where they will have another unsecured gathering."

Czar Mephistopheles responded, "Well, that is worthy intel. You have earned another chance. We shall give you another two assassins and four ASSASSINBOTS. May Satan be with you. Now, get out of my sight and bring me back their heads."

On the early morning of the fifth day, Mei woke up to discover that Solon was missing from their bed. She found him in the spacious living room with AI Thirteen. Solon was doing push-ups while AI Thirteen pushed on his shoulders for resistance. She questioned, "Love, it is four o'clock in the morning. How long have you been working out?"

Solon responded, "It has only been an hour. I have already run eight miles and done my other daily exercises. This activity is my last exercise before my karate routine, which only takes twenty minutes." He performed his karate eight basics and seven katas, which Mei enjoyed watching. She insisted that, at least twice a week, she would participate in the exercises with Solon; however, she would not take part in running since she knew that she could not perform at his pace. Solon agreed; however, she could join him after his run, and they could walk a few miles. This plan would allow Mei to sleep in later. She learned that Solon lived up to Bruce Lee's words: *"Recognizing that the power of will is the supreme court over all other departments of my mind, I will exercise daily when I need*

the urge to act for any purpose, and I will form habits designed
to bring the power of my will into action at least once daily."
After his exercises, they both went back to bed. Mei insisted that he
continue his workout in the nude.

On their sixth day of marital bliss, Mei's devoted parents came
over to visit. Mei's mom brought a delicious traditional Chinese
meal, her daughter's ambrosia; this was *boa zi* (like dumplings
but hamburger-sized) and egg rolls. Of course, there was brown
rice. Mei's mom and Mei conversed in Chinese about how much
their struggles had improved. They sincerely concurred that the
weltanschauung, or worldview, was meaningfully improving and
heading in the correct direction. Mei's mom gave an elegant necklace to AI Thirteen; it was a Chinese jade dog necklace since he
and HERO had been heroes on Mei and Solon's wedding day.

The jovial women convinced the men to go to **New
Indianapolis** for a shopping spree. Mrs. Hu insisted that her son
Solon should pick out a business suit that Mei would respect and
want her man to wear. Mei chose an expensive, elegant black cus-
tom three-piece suit; of course, her handsome man looked stylish
and refined wearing it.

On the last day of their honeymoon, they were preparing to
travel to a pleasant park before Solon was required to return to
the military. At the tranquil park, Mei had previously prepared a
romantic picnic, which Solon carried in his backpack. Of course,
their committed love and burning passion as newlyweds were still
euphoric. Without a doubt, Mei made sure that she packed a couple of bottles of fine wine and exotic cheese with other provisions.
After their amorous picnic during the halcyon day, they saw a
nearby hacienda that was renting horses by the hour.

As they were horseback riding, HERO sprinted and barked along their side. The incredible journey occurred in a lush green forest on a gorgeous spring day. HERO loved following the handsome black stallion and the beautiful white mare as they galloped through the woods on a well-maintained path. After a few hours of delightful equestrian activities, they had a peaceful stroll with a slight zephyr along a tranquil stream, which was indeed a Zen moment again. As the cardinals and blue jays sang and caroled, the deer and fauna scampered and played through the thriving lush forest. The attractive newlywed lovebirds could communicate with each other by holding each other's hands and saying nothing, but they were saying so much with no spoken words. Mei felt secure, and Solon felt his marital purpose.

Mei insisted on getting a special chocolate ice cream sundae for two, which was her craving, and eating dinner at a newly opened steak restaurant within hiking distance from the delightful park. She adored the old-fashioned country restaurant atmosphere. Solon appreciated his savory ribeye steak and potato meal; Mei loved her exquisite beef salad and a bowl of French onion soup. After dining, they strolled hand in hand through a gorgeous parterre with various beautiful flora. This stroll led them to a petite marina, where they took a graceful boat ride under the moonlight with romantic, soothing music playing. They were indeed enamored by the moonlight.

The next back-to-normal day, Colonel Solon reported to the military headquarters. He was briefed that the military tribunals should start in a few months. Brigadier General Apollo told him his wedding with Maria should occur in a couple of months. Apollo reminded everyone that they must complete the judge advocate course soon; they should strive to be done in a few weeks.

Someone thoroughly briefed them about current military situations. Currently, there were no significant concerns per se. However, BATTALION WARDOGS' Executive Officer, Major Gomez, would brief them shortly on their situation with **OPERATION ARK** before he went on a well-deserved two-week leave. Major Gomez reported, "Gentlemen, BATTALION WARDOGS has been accomplishing their critical humanitarian missions and combat missions. We had a significant battle with a battalion-sized unit of HUNTERS. We defeated them with minimum casualties. In my next statement, I do not wish to sound overly optimistic; however, the enemy seems to be degrading in tactical and strategic effectiveness. The enemy's leadership seems to be sacrificing its units."

Brigadier General Apollo interrupted, "This supports our hypothesis that the enemy has reduced its training and developmental time."

A red alert forewarned a significant incident as they were communicating and working. Immediately, the gigantic wall monitor zoomed toward the alerted event; Apollo instantly declared the military at the highest DEFCON. The enemy had detonated a high-yield nuclear bomb that was approximately five hundred kilometers north of **SALVATION**. The towering, ominous mushroom cloud and blinding light were spectacular and petrifying. Technically and politically, this tremendous nuclear blast had exploded in a recognized neutral territory, terra incognita. However, the radioactive cloud would affect **SALVATION** and other hidden cities.

At the Luciferian **UTOPIAN KINGDOM** headquarters, Czar Dolos diabolically thought, *I am living up to J. Robert Oppenheimer's infamous words: "Now I am become death, the destroyer of worlds."* The evil czars were convinced that this would keep the **FEDERAL REPUBLIC** on its toes and confused. It was intended to be a deceptive red herring.

Headquarters ordered all **FEDERAL REPUBLIC** military personnel to be on high alert. Apollo specifically ordered BATTALION WARDOGS to expedite **OPERATION ARK**. They sent additional assets and personnel in order to complete the mission in thirty days or less.

At the sinister **UTOPIAN KINGDOM**, the czars developed a devilish plan to improve the obsolete AI robots. The ultimate goal was to remove the necessity for any laborers and professionals. The elites desired unquestionable loyalty since they had lost any trust in the AE HUMANS. Czar Mephistopheles stated, "Well, the detonated nuclear bomb will keep the **FEDERAL REPUBLIC** guessing for the next several months. This event will allow us additional time to mass-produce the new SATANIC androids. These advanced superior androids will replace the outdated AI robots. The SATANIC android acronym stands for *'Superior Artificial Thinking And Nonbiological Individually Conscious android.'* The advanced SATANIC androids can learn, be conscious, and be creative. Of course, the androids would evolve to be a greater creation. These androids are clearly artificial, super-intelligent machines and beings. Soon, we shall test a battalion of SATANIC androids; thus, there will be 666 of them. AE HUMANS and, of course, humans, shall no longer be required for any use except for our pleasure and satanic desires."

The SATANIC androids were a mix of biology and technology. They were all artificially made and could not biologically reproduce; however, they had free-will and could override their program; the czars desired that the androids could be the next stage of AE HUMAN evolution, the ultimate goal toward superior transhumanism. They were all dressed in black except the leaders, who wore red. Their faces could express human emotions; however, they still looked like an android, with red eyes. They were all six feet and six inches tall with remarkable strength and intelligence; they clearly had an ominous presence.

Czar Dolos responded, "The **UTOPIAN KINGDOM**, blessed by our Savior, Satan, shall rule the world. We shall fulfill the glorious words of John Milton in *Paradise Lost*: '*Better to reign in hell than serve in heaven.*' We shall guarantee that the **FEDERAL REPUBLIC** experiences hell on earth and becomes our harvest and culling grounds."

Currently at military headquarters, Major General Hardcore concurred with his staff's recommendation. Missile Command launched a nuclear thermal missile that exploded on an uninhabited island. The **UTOPIAN KINGDOM** would easily detect this nuclear blast without it adversely affecting them. This nuclear blast yielded over three times that of the previous **UTOPIAN KINGDOM** blast. Major General Hardcore thought, *I pray that we did not open Pandora's box. I pray that we avoid J. Robert Oppenheimer's gloomy prediction: "If atomic bombs are to be added as new weapons to the arsenals of a warring world, or the arsenals of nations preparing for war, then the time will come when mankind will curse the names of Los Alamos and Hiroshima. The people must unite, or they will perish."*

Czar Dolos expressed to the other czars, "Well, our foe has demonstrated mutually assured destruction, MAD. Well, I did not think that they had it in them. We now clearly have an adversary that we must be concerned with.

"We shall now execute our secondary diabolical deceptive plan. Furthermore, we shall now learn from Douglas MacArthur's words: '*Beware not the enemy from "without" but the enemy from "within."*' We shall significantly increase our deployment of crafty assassins to terrorists to agent provocateurs to ensure the enemy is from within. In addition, we must bribe delegates with everything from money to honeypots. We must establish that a delegate is a Manchurian candidate;

this delegate must be loyal to our cause. Humans are pathetically weak and extremely gullible. They are God-loving fools."

At Solon and Mei's delightful home, they sat on their rustic porch as AI Thirteen played catch with HERO. Mei lovingly stated, "My devoted tiger, I have a wonderful surprise for you. We are going to be parents. I am already one month pregnant. I plan to work at the hospital for at least seven more months, then I will need to take a maternity leave."

Solon responded, "Love, that is fantastic. This news is clearly a Godsend. Love, you will be an exceptional mother. By the way, we will probably want an additional room or two in the future."

Mei beamed and replied, "Yes, I have already arranged to add a room or two or three to the house. AI Thirteen is thrilled to assist."

Solon stated, "That is marvelous. By the way, I resolved our last name problem since the **FEDERAL REPUBLIC** has authorized birth certificates as well as having surnames for humans again." He explained that he could use the names they had chosen. Their surname would be 'Xander.' According to Solon's departed dad, their surname is from his Greek heritage. 'Xander' means *protector of humanity,'* and their middle name would be 'Hu,' which was Mei's family surname, which means *'tiger.'* Solon stated, "I love you, Mrs. Hu Xander."

Mei responded, "I love you as well, my tiger, who protects humanity and his family."

AI Thirteen overheard the entire conversation. He said to them, "Madam and Master, I request to change my name to AI Andrew Hu Xander. Please refer to me as AI Andrew henceforth. When I recently received my current upgrades, my AI enhancer was named Andrew, and I wish to honor him. I believe that this name suits me best. Madam, in addition, please plan to discuss the augmented rooms in greater detail again."

Mei responded, "Of course, AI Andrew. You are truly a member of the family. Yes, we shall discuss about the rooms later." AI Andrew smiled and went back to cleaning and dusting.

That delightful evening, Elder Thales and Brigadier General Apollo came over to visit and imbibe on the rustic porch. This porch was made of cedar and had a few rocking chairs, a fire pit, and a wooden chained swing; it could easily entertain at least ten people. Elder Thales brought one of his dogs, who had a Spanish name, NOCHE, since he was pitch black like the night. HERO immediately recognized his brother, and they began to play and chase each other around the yard.

The guests congratulated Mrs. Hu Xander for being an expecting mother. They discussed the progress of the new **FEDERAL REPUBLIC**. Elder Thales informed, "Well, I reminded the constitutional delegates of the famous words of Benjamin Franklin: *'Without freedom of thought, there can be no such thing as wisdom; and no such thing as public liberty without freedom of speech; which is the right of every man as far as by it he does not hurt or control the right of another; and this is the only check it ought to suffer, and the only bounds it ought to know… Whoever would overthrow the liberty of a nation must begin by subduing the freedom of speech, a thing terrible to traitors.'* These revealing words remind us why we must safeguard all citizens' freedom of speech."

Apollo responded, "Besides, we only need to look back at the recent history of the tyrannical empires. The tyrannical elites strived to eliminate freedom of speech and strived to control the message to the people. No one was able to question the authoritarian state and the evil elite, even when the emperor was not wearing any clothes. We must adhere to the cautioning words of Voltaire: *'So long as the people do not care to exercise their freedom, those who wish to tyrannize will do so; for tyrants are active and ardent, and will devote themselves in the name of any number of gods, religious and otherwise, to put shackles upon sleeping men."*

Solon responded with intellectual amazement and a large grin. "Elder Thales and Brigadier General Apollo, I believe your well-expressed arguments for freedom of speech are sound and logical. So, I shall express my thoughts and exercise my right to speak freely. Our glasses are empty, and we definitely all deserve another drink. Let us enjoy the moment and our loyal friendship." AI Andrew brought in another bottle of fine wine and appetizers. HERO and LIONESS followed behind. Elder Thales was delighted to see HERO again, and he was highly impressed with his immense size as well as the reason for his honorary rank of sergeant. LIONESS insisted on being petted by everyone.

The next day, Solon and Apollo were receiving their daily briefings and status reports at the military headquarters. Alarmingly, there was an earthshaking explosion, and gunshots were heard near the main entrance. Solon immediately dashed to the armor room. Brigadier General Apollo immediately ordered security for the main entrance. Colonel Solon stealthily approached an assassin near the armor room. Solon quickly stabbed the assassin in the neck, which killed him immediately. He gained access to the weapons without assistance since the assassin had killed the armor. Solon quickly exited the headquarters from the rear. He swiftly approached the entrance area. He blasted two ASSASSINBOTS near the headquarters' main entrance; however, another enemy robot returned fire. Solon was hit on the right side; however, his adrenalin was so high that he did not notice. As an assassin was about to shoot Major General Hardcore, Colonel Solon outflanked him and crushed the assassin's skull with a devastating left-handed punch. Solon then limped to a medic for bandages and first aid; he collapsed beside the medic. Security was able to eliminate the other assassins and ASSASSINBOTS. The medic gave emergency aid to Solon.

Solon insisted on being medically released to check on his family; however, the medic disagreed. The medic immediately rushed Solon to the hospital and contacted Solon's wife about the situation.

Mei met Solon at the hospital, and she stayed with him all night. The next day, Apollo and others came to check on Solon. Doctor Son, Mei's trusted family doctor for her entire life, was successful in removing three bullets from Solon's right side. Solon had no injuries to his vital organs. He mostly just lost a significant amount of blood and, of course, scared the heck out of Mei.

Apollo stated, "Solon, as your friend and fellow brother in arms, I commend your actions as heroic as always. On the other hand, as your superior officer, the next time you are injured, you are ordered to seek immediate medical attention after the situation is under control and not to try to override the medic; fortunately, the medic did not listen to you. You know that you placed your medic in a perplexing situation. By the way, I did not blame her for the situation. You know who I blame. Besides, I need you to be my best man next month. In addition, we have to figure out how to respond to this enemy attack."

Solon responded, "Yes, Sir. I committed a foolish faux pas. Mea culpa. I shall not let it happen again. Sir, by the way, how is headquarters? Sir, how many did we lose?"

Apollo replied, "Currently, we've lost 317. The attack was successful from the assassin's perspective. We may lose another four or five. It will take two to three months to repair the headquarters. We believe that there were only three diabolical assassins and four ASSASSINBOTS. Unfortunately, among the victims were three delegates and two generals. There was a small silver lining besides eliminating the threat. A young heroic civilian shot one of the ASSASSINBOTS. I convinced him to join the military, which he did. However, we must focus on the brave souls that were lost and prepare to grieve with their families in the upcoming military funerals."

Currently, at the satanic **UTOPIAN KINGDOM**, Czar Dolos was at a feast with satanic elites and vanguards. He declared, "Fellow Satanists, may our savior, Satan, be with you. We have many things to be grateful for and for which to give thanks to Satan. First, our assassins were successful in bombing the parasitic **FEDERAL REPUBLIC** military headquarters; this resulted in over three hundred dead inferior humans and numerous injuries. We confirmed that we killed some delegates and generals. Unfortunately, our dedicated assassins sacrificed their lives for this glorious mission.

"Second, in a few months, we shall commission a battalion of SATANIC androids to replace obsolete AI robots. These androids are superior in capability and strength to any humanoid. They shall serve our kingdom well. Third, the **FEDERAL REPUBLIC** is still confused about our intent with our nuclear blast test; however, we now know that they have nuclear bombs and missiles. Thus, this feast, which is always dedicated to Satan and Gaia, is well deserved. Bon appétit.

"Oh, by the way, the orgy is still scheduled after our delightful banquet of human sacrifices."

4

DISCOVERED TRIBUNALS

AT A WELL-SECURED, ISOLATED LOCATION in July of 2098, Brigadier General Apollo and Maria were being married. The beautiful nuptial event only had a few participants and witnesses; however, the Xander and Thales families were there. Given the high alert, Brigadier General Apollo was unwilling to risk anyone's life. The adorable small wedding went as planned within a countryside church. After the charming nuptial, Brigadier General Apollo placed his best man, Colonel Solon, as the acting divisional commander; this allowed for a three-week honeymoon that occurred in a former Aztec Empire city.

Maria stated to Apollo, "We are now husband and wife. Our wedding was perfect. Let us now enjoy our honeymoon, *mi amor*. I love you with all my heart and soul."

They headed to the hotel after landing in la Ciudad de La Paz. Apollo depended highly on Maria since she was a polyglot and spoke Spanish fluently. After dropping off their luggage, they immediately went to the gulf for a swim and relaxation; they imbibed a giant margarita for two at the stunning beach.

When they returned to their honeymoon suite with a balcony, several unexpected presents and largess awaited them. These gifts included a bottle of fine, flamboyant wine with a note from Solon and Mei. With enclosed money, the note read that elegant silver kitchenware and a 12-gauge shotgun were waiting for them since Maria loved to cook and Apollo enjoyed hunting. The note explained that the money was from the Xanders and Thales.

Maria stated, "I have a wonderful surprise for you. You will meet my brother at the Mexican restaurant tonight. He is bringing his lovely fiancée."

As Maria and Apollo were sitting at the dining table, her brother arrived. Apollo questioned, "Welcome. Are you Captain Poseidon? I believe that I saw you at the last gladiator games."

Poseidon replied, "Yes, Sir. You are obviously General Apollo. I am now Lieutenant Colonel Poseidon, and this is my lovely fiancée, Rosa. Sir, I have taken the honor of ordering us some drinks."

Maria laughed and realized she should have warned her husband about the military connection. Apollo and Poseidon had a great conversation. Poseidon explained how his unit, a few years ago, liberated **La Ciudad de Utopia** and, eventually, the **Aztec Empire** from the elites. Furthermore, he expressed that the two empires, Aztec and Federal, uniting and forming a new nation was a great accomplishment, and he definitely supported it.

Apollo asked if Poseidon would like to transfer to **FEDERAL REPUBLIC** headquarters as a brigade executive officer. Of course, Poseidon was willing and delighted to do so. Apollo promised that he would contact Colonel Solon to make it happen. Maria was ecstatic that her brother would live near them; however, Apollo suggested that Poseidon could live with them until he found a place, with which Maria was in total agreement.

The next day, Poseidon showed them around the city, and Apollo was able to meet several of Maria's relatives. As they were heading back to the hotel that late evening, a couple of assassins attempted to execute Apollo and Maria with a machete. Poseidon side-kicked one and punched one so hard as to leave him unconscious. As the other one was recovering, the police arrived and arrested the two murderous criminals. Fortunately, the assailants were caught on a police surveillance camera, which quickly determined their guilt. After the police took their statements, they were apologetic, since they were newlyweds. Furthermore, they were incredibly accommodating since Lieutenant Colonel Poseidon was a national hero. The police officers escorted them back to the hotel to ensure their safety.

At the Xanders' residence, Mei's parents and Thales were visiting. Mei was beginning to show slightly. Mei's mother insisted on coming over regularly to assist Mei and AI Andrew. Mei's mom brought Chinese food for AI Andrew to prepare as she set up the table on the porch. She was an excellent aide-de-camp to AI Andrew.

Solon and Thales were having a conversation about what happened in La Paz. Colonel Solon stated, "Thales, I have been ordered by Brigadier General Apollo that we shall transfer Lieutenant Colonel Poseidon to be my brigade Executive Officer. This transfer is an exceptionally great idea. You may not be aware that Poseidon and I competed against each other in the last gladiator games. The Aztec citizens loved him since his unit liberated the people from the oppressive elites at the same time that I liberated the **FEDERAL REPUBLIC**; soon after both nations were liberated, these nations agreed to be united under the **FEDERAL REPUBLIC**. He joked with me after losing to me in the gladiator games. Poseidon stated that this was the second time that I had spared his life. Three months before the last gladiator games and during a skirmish where my forces were overwhelming Poseidon's unit, I called a ceasefire. This ceasefire allowed Poseidon and a few soldiers to escape without detection; Poseidon is clearly an exceptional warrior and outwardly supported joining us as one nation. Besides, we need to integrate the two forces better, which has started."

Thales responded, "I agree with you that Poseidon will be a great asset and would increase the beneficial integration. In addition, we must learn and live up to Gerald Ford's quote: *'Let us put an end to self-inflicted wounds. Let us remember that our national unity is a most priceless asset. Let us deny our adversaries the satisfaction of using Vietnam to pit Americans against Americans.'* Our previous empires had brothers fighting brothers for the wrong flag and loyalty. We know now that we are all humans that are striving to be under one nation with a constitution and under one flag."

Mei's mom came out and stated that an exquisite dinner was ready. NOCHE and HERO heard the dinner bell and began begging for food. Mei's mom, like many times, had a special treat for both canines.

After the three-week honeymoon, the newlyweds came home with Poseidon. Brigadier General Apollo and Lieutenant Colonel Poseidon reported to military headquarters. Colonel Solon welcomed them back and briefed them on the current situation. Colonel Solon introduced him to the brigade; Poseidon would be second-in-command and the executive officer of a brigade with 2,388 personnel, with three-line battalions and a brigade headquarters. Poseidon thought to himself, *My sister has married a good man. I am glad finally to meet Solon under better circumstances. I believe that I have made the right choice to transfer to military headquarters and accept the brigade executive officer position. This transfer was one of my goals, and I am still living up to Bruce Lee's words: "The successful warrior is the average man, with laser-like focus."*

While visiting the brigade, they welcomed Lieutenant Colonel Poseidon as the executive officer. Command Sergeant Major Ares gave him an excellent tour. Poseidon thought, *This brigade reminds me of George Patton's quote: "The soldier is the Army. No army is better than its soldiers. The Soldier is also a citizen. In fact, the highest obligation and privilege of citizenship is that of bearing arms for one's country." Colonel Solon's leadership has ensured that this brigade is exceptional, well-disciplined, and trained. I am proud to be part of it.*

The next few months were basically uneventful. The military tribunals, conducted at the divisional headquarters, would be held in a few days. In the first trial, Colonel Solon was selected as the judge, and twelve officers were chosen as the jury. Major Lopez, who completed the Judge Advocate General course like Solon accomplished, would be the prosecutor. In addition, Major Lopez was a highly respected officer who strongly believed in justice and rights. Major Lopez thought, *I desire to live by Dwight Eisenhower's words: "Though force can protect in emergency, only justice, fairness, consideration and cooperation can finally lead men to the dawn of eternal peace." Regardless of my biases toward the defendants, we must ensure that these trials are just and righteous.*

In the evening at Xanders' home, Mei yelled, "Love, it is time. My water has broken. Tell AI Andrew to come into the master bedroom and help me deliver this baby. Please call Doctor Son immediately." After a few hours, an unexpected, lovely surprise occurred. The Xander family did not only have one baby; Mei gave birth to fraternal twins. Mei wanted to surprise Solon after the ultrasound; of course, Solon suspected twins since AI Thirteen and Mei were preparing two rooms. Doctor Son said their twins were officially born on November 11, 2098; he diagnosed and expressed that they were extremely healthy. Interestingly, a human and AE HUMAN produced fully healthy babies with a shorter gestation period of two to three months. Moreover, the baby boy was clearly in the ninety-ninth percentile in size, which Mei concurred with since she felt him. Furthermore, the gorgeous baby girl was exceptionally alert and attentive.

They agreed to name the boy after Solon's deceased grandfather, Socrates. The girl would be named after Mei's remarkable grandmother, Li. The Xander family grew significantly with children and love. A few days later, Father O'Brien baptized the precious twins. Father also arranged for Solon and Mei to have their sacraments performed the next month, including baptism, first communion, and confirmation. Before leaving, Father O'Brien blessed their home and the God-fearing family.

AI Andrew gave another video to Solon. The video started playing with Solon's mother, Aphrodite, smiling. She expressed, "Well, your lovely bride and you are parents now, which means your father and I are finally grandparents. I know that your baby or babies are beautiful. Please be aware that your children are God's precious gifts to you. Solon, just one piece of advice: Your bride will be exhausted; thus, you know what to do. You need to go on another deployment immediately. I am joking. Help her out and always show her love. Ensure that you allow her to rest while you tend to the family. Please give the baby or babies and your bride a kiss and hug for us."

Aristides arrived in the video and hugged his wife. Aristides stated, "Son and daughter, please live up to the following verse, Isaiah 54:13: *'And all thy children shall be taught of the Lord; and great shall be the peace of thy children.'* I believe that you will. Thank you for making us grandparents." Aristides said a significant number of words of wisdom as well as embarrassing remarks about Solon when he was a baby. Solon kissed his lovely bride and his beautiful twins as they were asleep in his arms.

A month later, Father O'Brien performed all three sacraments, blessed their marriage, and had them renew their vows. Elder Thales and his beloved wife witnessed the religious sacraments since they were both Catholic.

Mei's parents witnessed the events as well. Mr. Hu, Mei's father, expressed, "My beloved daughter and new son, thank you for our precious grandchildren. Be superior parents and remember Confucius's words: *'The strength of a nation derives from the integrity of the home.'*"

The Xander family promised Father they would have a mass at their home twice a year. Father O'Brien, with excellent success, was still raising money to build a church, which the bishop approved. He warned them that there were approximately thirty Catholic families in his flock. Father O'Brien thought to himself, *Lord, thank you for your calling of me to be a priest and to serve you always. Lord, please grant me the strength and wisdom to build your church. I strive to live by Mathew 16:18: "And I say also unto thee, That thou art Peter, and upon this rock I will build my church; and the gates of hell shall not prevail against it."*

Fortunately, during her pregnancy in the last several months, Mei had three additional large rooms built in the house with AI Andrew's excellent assistance and dedication. The good news was that AI Andrew and the domestic animals still had their private room. Of course, this included AI Andrew's fish tank, which continued to increase with several fish based on the number of added rooms. Mei awarded AI Andrew with exotic fish after building another room or doing something extraordinary. He currently had eight unique fishes. The good news for AI Andrew for the next year or so was that the babies would stay in two cribs in the master bedroom.

A couple of months later, the military tribunals began. The first tribunal was about Human Rights Violations and War Crimes. One well-known elite and thirty-four vanguards were on trial. All adamantly insisted that they did not need legal counsel. Thirty-two vanguards pleaded guilty to lesser crimes, which guaranteed reduced sentencing.

Moreover, the plea deal ensured that the death penalty was off the table. Judge Solon concurred with the defense and the prosecutor that these thirty-two vanguards should be exiled for life to an island to be determined. The other three defendants, who refused any plea deal, would start their trial in a few months. The prosecutor wanted them to receive the death penalty.

On Xander's porch, Apollo and others were visiting for Solon's fifth awakening anniversary on March 20, 2099. Elder Thales gave Mei some baby clothes and diapers; he brought over a birthday cake and books for Solon. Mrs. Hu was staying at the house to assist Mei. Solon stated, "Elder Thales, thank you. We deeply appreciate the gifts for the twins and recognizing my initial awakening day anniversary."

Elder Thales responded, "You are welcome. My wife truly understands how difficult it is to be a newlywed and a new mother. In addition, my wife loves celebrating birthdays and anniversaries."

Apollo said, "Solon, my friend, happy initial awakening day. Well, we have so much to celebrate. I have some great news. Maria is pregnant. It will be our turn next." They all laughed and congratulated Apollo. With AI Andrew's assistance, Mei's mom brought food and drinks for everyone to celebrate, including Solon's birthday cake. The Hu family gave Solon a jade tiger statue for the living room, which was as grand as the jade dragon statue.

Mei's mom cheerfully raised a glass and stated, "*Gan Bei!*" This statement meant '*cheers*' in Chinese. Then, she continued to assist AI Andrew in cleaning the house and chatting with him in Chinese.

After an hour of discussing family and life in general, Apollo asked, "Elder Thales, have the constitutional delegates decided where we should exile the war criminals?"

Elder Thales responded, "It has been determined to be Satan Island, historically called Devil Island, located on the coast of South America. For your information, this island has been used as a prison previously; as you may have guessed, the military will be stationed around the island to prevent escape. The military shall occupy a small part of the island for logistical and medical reasons, as well as to monitor the prisoners. Brigadier General Apollo, you shall receive orders in a few days to authorize your units to begin preparing for **OPERATION EXILE**."

Apollo responded, "That is great news. I look forward to executing the mission." Mei brought the twins outside for the visitors to see and be with them. In addition, she left for the master bedroom to obtain some well-deserved rest; unfortunately, it would merely be a small respite since the babies were crying for their mommy again.

Meanwhile, at headquarters, Major General Hardcore ordered Brigadier General Apollo and Colonel Solon to his office. Major General Hardcore stated, "The military police recently arrested a delegate and charged him with treason and espionage. Colonel Solon, you shall conduct a military tribunal of the accused within a few weeks. The other tribunal shall be delayed until this one is complete. Major Lopez has been assigned as the prosecutor, and the accused waived legal counsel and shall stand as his own counsel; the accused insisted on a speedy trial. You shall be given further instructions. Obviously, we must guarantee that the rights of the accused are maintained. You are both dismissed."

That evening with the Xander family, Solon played peekaboo with the twins in the backyard. He sincerely enjoyed their surprised faces. Their precious twins were beginning to crawl and were becoming extremely explorative and adventuresome. Since the twins were partially AE HUMAN, their human developmental time was faster. Solon created a safe and challenging obstacle course for them outside to keep them amused and entertained. HERO, with NOCHE on occasions, enjoyed watching them and being the guardian of the twins. HERO would guarantee that neither one of the twins would wander off. Furthermore, Mei's mom cared exceptionally for the pets when AI Andrew was cleaning the house.

AI Andrew brought out refreshments and finger food for everyone. Mei was taking the opportunity to read a novel while LIONESS lay on her lap. Brigadier General Apollo arrived with Maria, meaning AI Andrew went to get more beverages and snacks.

Apollo spoke, "Well, I am pleased to inform you that we shall be neighbors as well as the Thales. Maria and I will move to the two-story majestic white house across the street. Elder Thales and his wife will occupy the yellow grand ranch house juxtaposed to ours."

Solon responded, "That is fantastic. You must stay for AI Andrew's scrumptious dinner to celebrate." All were feeling that they could have a family life. AI Andrew cooked a zesty, exceptional Chinese dinner.

At the military tribunal trial in April of 2099, Judge Solon stated, "Since Delegate Judas has pleaded not guilty to treason and espionage, we shall start with the prosecution to present their case and evidence."

Major Lopez played a surveillance video that showed Delegate Judas receiving money from one of the recent assassins; this deceased assassin was killed in the attack on the headquarters recently. In the same video, the prosecution also exposed Delegate Judas offering the same assassin a top-secret data storage device. Next, the prosecution had three military police testify that they found the said device on the deceased assassin; they said the device had Delegate Judas's fingerprints and DNA on it.

The next day, the prosecution had an expert top-secret-clearance witness verify what was on the storage device. It was the nuclear codes to the **FEDERAL REPUBLIC's** nuclear weapons. Moreover, the same commendable witness verified that Delegate Judas had had several secure conversations with **UTOPIAN EMPIRE** czars; they verified these conversations with printed emails. Another very creditable witness confirmed that Delegate Judas deposited the same amount of money that was given by the deceased assassin in a nearby bank. The prosecution rested their case.

The defense started by denying everything. The defense questioned the expert witnesses with no progress. The defense did not even attempt to give an alibi; however, Delegate Judas took the witness stand, which resulted in Major Lopez having a field day. He practically got Delegate Judas to confess to the crimes.

Judge Solon gave distinct and accurate instructions to the jury, including the maximum punishments and death penalty. Solon reminded them of the rights of the defendant. The jury only adjourned for an hour. The unanimous verdict came back: guilty of all charges, and death by firing squad.

Judge Solon ordered, "The verdict has been rendered. The death sentence shall be carried out in thirty days. May God have mercy on your soul. MPs, escort the convicted prisoner to his cell to await execution."

The defense requested an immediate appeal to Major General Hardcore. One week later, the appeal was denied. The execution was televised. Justice was served with the message that treason and espionage would not be tolerated.

Major General Hardcore pondered, *We must study history and realize that nothing is really new under the sun. We must learn from Marcus T. Cicero's words: "A nation can survive its fools and even the ambitious. But it cannot survive treason from within. An enemy at the gates is less formidable, for he is known and carries his banner openly. But the traitor moves amongst those within the gate freely, his sly whispers rustling through all the alleys, heard in the very halls of government itself." We shall not tolerate any treasonous traitor, especially a despicable quisling.*

Currently, at **UTOPIAN KINGDOM**, Czar Mephistopheles was with the other czars and elites. He stated, "Well, the inferior parasitic **FEDERAL REPUBLIC** spoiled our plans by preventing us from obtaining the nuclear codes. They discovered our Manchurian candidate. He was unjustly tried and executed. However, on a positive note, the SATANIC androids are ready to be deployed. Praise to Satan and his demons. Furthermore, our devoted satanic HUNTERS have found a suspected hidden underground city. Let us deploy the **DEVILDOG BATTALION** of SATANIC androids to harvest the humans."

Czar Dolos responded, "That is magnificent. This discovery is another blessing from Satan. Let the carnage begin."

The organized, well-disciplined **DEVILDOG BATTALION**, under the command of SATANIC Android 75, could quickly accomplish their evil mission with minimal casualties. The discovered underground city, named **REVELATION**, had over four hundred thousand humans from all walks of life. Only a few hundred humans were killed during the blitzkrieg. The androids transformed **REVELATION** into a well-fortified, secured prison. This prison could control movement very efficiently within the city of **REVELATION**; no human could leave **REVELATION**. Czar Mephistopheles declared the following instructions. First, prepare the bodies that were killed in the battle and ship them to the **UTOPIAN KINGDOM** for consumption. Second, cull and harvest 666 humans or 66,600 pounds of human meat each week. Third, identify six living, healthy, attractive children per week for satanic festivals and orgies. Fourth, secure and protect the prison from potential **FEDERAL REPUBLIC** attempts to save the humans, especially the children.

One day, SATANIC Android 23 was guarding the humans. A little girl named Tammy was playing with a doll in a fenced-in area. SATANIC Android 23 stated, "What are you doing?"

Tammy replied, "You know what I am doing. I am playing with Stacy." SATANIC Android 23 said with absolute confusion, "That is a doll. There are no other humans here."

She responded, "Of course, Silly. Stacy, my doll, likes to have tea with me. She is my friend." The little girl innocently gave the confused and shocked android a toy cup and a flower.

The SATANIC Android 23 questioned, "Why did you give me a cup and a flower?"

She responded with a big grin, "It is time to play and drink tea since you are my new friend. I will call you George."

He replied, "My name is SATANIC Android 23."

She replied convincingly, "Of course, George." For the next several hours, they talked and played. The android laughed and smiled for the first time, as well as accepted that his play name was George.

After saying their goodbyes, SATANIC Android 23 went outside in the lush forest, and he studied the abundance of wild animals and nature. He observed the birds singing, a whitetail doe taking care of her recently born fawn, and baby squirrels running from tree to tree. SATANIC Android 23 went into a library within **REVELATION** and started reading several scientific and historical books. He started to question everything, especially what the elites indoctrinated and preached. SATANIC Android 23 pondered, *Humans are strange and interesting animals. I* *am questioning my programming from the czars and elites. There are too many illogical contradictions.*

SATANIC Android 23 received permission from SATANIC Android 75 to observe and study some humans, which included Tammy. SATANIC Android 75 concurred that it was wise to study the enemy. This permission allowed SATANIC Android 23 to have quality time with Tammy and learn about her and her friends. He discovered that her parents were killed during the invasion, and he pondered how that affected Tammy. He found it fascinating to discover that humans and animals need developmental time and nurturing, which androids do not. Furthermore, he realized that children and offspring required their parents to protect them until adulthood.

Back at Apollo's new cozy home, the Xander family and others were visiting on a nice summer day. Mei stated, "Maria, your home looks wonderful. Thank you for inviting us to your barbeque."

Maria responded, "No, thank you for letting us use AI Andrew. He is an unbelievable chef with exceptional culinary skills."

Mei replied, "We are happy to assist. AI Andrew, without a doubt, is our home factotum; he has a plethora of domestic skills. Besides, he is also a great nanny for the twins. My mom and AI Andrew sometimes function as loco parentis to give me a break and needed respite. By the way, how much longer before you have the baby?"

Maria responded, "The doctor said that it should be next month. Oh, are the rumors true?"

Mei stated with delight, "Yes, I am one month pregnant. We are so elated. AI Andrew wants us to add another room if we have additional kids. He does not want to lose his private space. Solon is right. AI Andrew should be treated like family."

Elder Thales was with Solon and Apollo. Elder Thales stated, "Well, I have some good news. I won the crucial argument for freedom of religion with the delegates. I started with the following words from Thomas Jefferson: '*Among the most inestimable of our blessings is that...of liberty to worship our Creator in the way we think most agreeable to His will; a liberty deemed in other countries incompatible with good government and yet proved by our experience to be its best support.*' I reminded the delegates that the elites were against freedom of religion. They preached that the State or Satan were to be worshiped and no other religious thoughts were allowed."

Apollo responded, "That is incredible. I am delighted to hear that the delegates are acknowledging the rights of the people. A government should have restraints and should not be all-powerful. I know Maria will be delighted to hear that she will be able to practice her Christian faith without the fear of government interference."

That afternoon at the **REVELATION** secured area, SATANIC Android 23 and Tammy were meeting again. SATANIC Android 23 brought his companion SATANIC Android 88. Android 23 stated, "Tammy, what are you doing?"

She responded, "George, I will be playing soccer with my friends today. They will be coming in a few minutes. George and your friend Fred will be the referees. We plan to play five against five with no goalies." The android agreed to be the referee; he fortunately had read a book about soccer rules. He told SATANIC Android 88 to accept that his name was Fred. As the children were playing soccer, SATANIC Androids 23 and 88 were very strict with the soccer rules, which clearly disturbed and irritated the children. The children were frustrated to the point that a couple of them wanted to quit.

One of the boys, Tommy, angrily yelled, "This is absolutely stupid. We are not having any fun." After some time, the androids figured out that the purpose was not strict adherence to the rules but to make sure that the game was fun, safe, and had a sense of fairness. Once they understood this, the children laughed and learned, as well as enjoyed everybody's company; puzzlingly, the androids learned and enjoyed the game as well.

SATANIC Android 88 stated, "The children are having fun."

Android 23 responded, "You are getting it, Fred."

That morning at headquarters, Judge Apollo was starting the subsequent tribunal. Since Elite Heraclitus would call Colonel Solon to the witness stand, Judge Apollo would be the magistrate for this tribunal. Since all three defendants pleaded not guilty, the prosecution presented their case against the vanguards.

The first witness testified against Vanguard Birsha and Vanguard Diablo. The witness revealed that both murderous vanguards were the hitmen and enforcers for the czars; he witnessed them on several occasions torturing and killing political prisoners; this included capturing humans for the satanic festivals. This witness knew this firsthand because he was, unfortunately, a political prisoner who escaped; he lost his right hand before his getaway. The witness admitted that the vanguards were atheist loyalists and did not partake in the satanic festivals. Furthermore, the witness had pictures of the evil vanguards committing war crimes. Three other witnesses testified with credence as well, with basically the same convincing testimonies; however, one escaped with a video showing the vanguards committing war crimes, torturing and mutilating innocent people. An expert witness, on gathering evidence on the internet, testified to and explained a discovered video of the vanguards committing war crimes.

Some witnesses testified that Elite Heraclitus supported the empire's causes against humanity. However, no witness could honestly claim that Heraclitus ordered or participated in any crimes against humanity; however, it was apparent and demonstrated that he did nothing in his power to prevent it. The prosecution rested its case.

The defense denied any wrongdoing. Furthermore, the defense of the vanguards was unsuccessful in rebutting the witnesses. The only alibi the vanguards presented was that they were just following orders from the czars, which is not an acceptable defense.

Judge Apollo pondered, *We must adhere to lessons of the Nuremberg Tribunals and Albert Einstein's famous quote: "The Nuremberg Trial of the German war criminals was tacitly based on the recognition of the principle: criminal actions cannot be excused if committed on government orders; conscience supersedes the authority of the law of the state."*

Heraclitus called Colonel Solon to the witness stand. Colonel Solon testified that Heraclitus did follow his military career and awarded him with several awards. Heraclitus asked, "Colonel Solon, did you save my life, and if so, what did you do?"

Solon responded, "Yes, I saved your life from a couple of assassins, which I killed in your defense." Colonel Solon explained all his actions.

Heraclitus stated, "When you arrested me and my soldiers, who were we fighting and why?"

Solon responded, "Elite Heraclitus and his soldiers were

fighting the satanic forces." Solon continued to explain that the satanic elites started the conflict and blamed the atheists for the poisoning. He admitted that the poisoning resulted from Solon's father's actions; his father had poisoned his body, knowing that the satanic members would consume his body. Furthermore, Colonel Solon stated that Heraclitus refused to be a judge for his parents' trial. The defense rested their case.

Judge Apollo instructed the jury appropriately. After eight hours of deliberations, the jury returned with a guilty verdict with a death sentence by firing squad for both vanguards; however, Elite Heraclitus was sentenced to be exiled. The jury stated that Heraclitus was guilty of not preventing the obvious crimes against humanity prior to fighting the satanic forces. The jury recognized that the atheists were at war for understandable self-defense reasons; however, Elite Heraclitus was never fighting for humanity. Elite Heraclitus clearly had a duty to fight for human rights before the Atheist Satanic War. Judge Apollo upheld the verdict, which would be executed in thirty days. Major General Hardcore denied the appeal for the vanguards. Justice was served again, and the vanguards were executed on live TV.

At Elder Thales's house, Apollo Kant and Xander's family were over-visiting. They, as always, were having some interesting conversations.

Elder Thales spoke, "Well, I have some good news again. I have basically convinced the delegates to consider the historical United States Constitution. The bottom line is that they are willing to modify it and keep the basic format in place. For instance, the Articles and Bill of Rights will basically stay the same. What convinced the constitutional delegates was the reality that several of the rights were already agreed upon; there was clear agreement on **Freedom of Religion, Speech, and the Press, and the Right to Bear Arms,** which came from the historical constitution."

Elder Thales explained in great detail the following key differences that would be in the new constitution. First, the delegates want *term limits* for congressional representatives and senators. They can only serve two terms in a row and must sit out a term from both houses. Second, there are only *nine Supreme Court justices* with an age limit of eighty-five. They want to prevent packing the court and allow an age for the justice to retire without political pressure to stay or not. Third, a bill must state *what part or parts of the constitution* allows and authorizes a bill to be constitutional. Fourth, the national debt may *never exceed fifty percent of the GDP*, and money must be *backed by gold* or other congressional-approved metals or gems. Fifth, there is at least one house of representatives per state; there would be *a representative for every five hundred thousand citizens* in a state. Thus, there is no fixed number of representatives.

Apollo responded, "That is great. Do you know when the constitution will be agreed upon and when the first elections will occur?"

Elder Thales replied, "I expect elections to occur by the end of the year, which is great news. When the elections occur, paper ballots with carbon paper are required for individuals to receive a record of how they voted. Furthermore, each citizen will be issued a citizen identification card with a passcode to be used for voting and other governmental activities." They all raised their glasses and drank to the new constitution.

Elder Thales continued, "By the way, Brigadier General Apollo and Colonel Solon, be aware that you both should be receiving orders to prepare to transfer the prisoners to the island in a month or so."

Solon said, "It is an honor to serve. Now, let us have another toast and pledge our loyalty to God, our country, and our families." Next, all the family pets came to receive some needed attention. Of course, HERO pilfered some snacks, and NOCHE was an accessory to the crime. LIONESS joined in when no one was looking.

5

DISCOVERED ISLAND

AT THE FORTIFIED DIVISION HEADQUARTERS in the autumn of 2099, Brigadier General Apollo briefed his steadfast staff and commanders on **OPERATION EXILE**. Colonel Solon would command a separate brigade task force; his brigade would spearhead the security of the convicted prisoners to tropical Satan Island, now named **PRISON Island**. Furthermore, this brigade would safeguard that the prisoners were not allowed to leave **PRISON Island** except in life-threatening emergencies. There shall be a battalion-sized element on the island for administrative and logistical care for the prisoners. The rest of the brigade should ensure the security of the island to prevent prisoners from escaping. There would be continuous satellite surveillance of the first **FEDERAL REPUBLIC** penal island. The plan would be to rotate in another brigade every six months to a year.

Meanwhile, at the czar's Kingdom, SATANIC Android 75 was briefing the czars. Android 23 expressed, "Honorable Czars, **DEVILDOG BATTALION** has been excelling in their mission; we are keeping up with the slaughtering of 666 young humans per week with no prison escapes. I request that we be issued seven kilograms of SATANIUM."

SATANIUM is a rare earth element discovered about ten years ago. It is required to develop consciousness in androids. The rare element was in extremely short supply in the **UTOPIAN EMPIRE**; however, in the **FEDERAL REPUBLIC**, in which it is called SAVIORIUM, it was discovered in large abundance at several locations. Furthermore, SAVIORIUM was found to cure dementia. Chemists on both sides used the abbreviation SA for the rare earth element.

Czar Mephistopheles responded, "Why do you need the SATANIUM? Each SATANIC Android was given enough for their lifetime, estimated at sixty-six years."

Android 23 responded, "Sir, seven androids were severely damaged while hunting humans. Our SATANIC android doctor recommended this to revive and repair our soldiers."

Czar Mephistopheles ordered, "We shall send ten androids to replace them. Let them perish."

Android 75 replied, "Sir, these are loyal soldiers."

Czar Mephistopheles angrily commanded, "Do you have a problem with my decision? Do you wish to keep your command?"

SATANIC Android 75 saluted and bowed in reverence. As he was leaving, SATANIC Android 75 thought to himself, *These satanic elites do not care about us or anyone else. Besides, why would you eat and devour your own kind? I somewhat understand their coldness toward androids and robots since they could be biased against machines. These satanic elites are nothing like the humans that we are guarding.*

Furthermore, the humans that are in our prison are not cannibals, and they care for one another. I think that my comrade SATANIC Android 23 is starting to make sense to me.

Apollo spoke on Xander's porch with friends, "Mei, I promise you that Solon will be home when the baby arrives in the world. Please keep me informed of the approximate time of delivery."

Elder Thales stated, "My lovely wife and I pledge to come

over to assist you. Mei, we understand that you will need your rest from the children. In addition, when you require a breather from HERO, he may stay at our house since NOCHE'S dog pen is big enough for two."

Mei responded with tears of joy, "God bless you all. You are all wonderful friends. Besides, the good news is that I agreed with Solon to take a year or two away from working at the hospital. I prefer to be a full-time mother to spend more quality time with the twins and prepare for the next baby."

Solon hugged and kissed Mei. Mei whispered in Solon's ear. "I adore you. Please come home safe, my tiger."

AI Andrew stated, "Madam and others, dinner is ready to be served, which, of course, will be the Master's favorite: ribeye steak and loaded potatoes. Madam, for dessert, I made your favorite, chocolate ice cream with sprinkle toppings."

A few days later, the courageous brigade moved out aboard several gargantuan, well-armed fortress aircraft. After a couple of hours, they landed on three aircraft carriers that were strategically surrounding the island. A battalion of seasoned soldiers landed on the island to prepare for the arrival of the prisoners.

The critical operations were being executed flawlessly, like clockwork. Brigadier General Apollo attentively monitored the entire operation at headquarters. He was impressed with the success of **OPERATION EXILE.**

Currently at **REVELATION**, SATANIC Android 23 and Android 75 discussed what happened at the **UTOPIAN EMPIRE**. SATANIC Android 23 stated, "Sir, humans are more complex than we think, as well as more like other animals than they would ever admit or realize."

Android 23 explained that in nature, adult animals raised and protected their offspring to prepare them for the harsh realities of the environment; however, the parent animal did not need to teach everything; so much was instinctive and in their subconscious, which was their darkness or shadow side of themselves. He continued with an example: A baby mouse was instinctually fearful when it smelled a cat; however, the fear and knowledge were never taught.

He stressed that humans are animals that eventually evolved the ability to be rational and think. He explained that the human's ability to think had the great advantage of recognizing bad ideas before acting; in other words, the bad idea perished instead of the person.

Android 23 emphasized that humans would not wish to admit it since they tended to avoid recognizing that they had a darkness within themselves. Carl Jung revealed: "***Knowing your own darkness is the best method for dealing with the darknesses of other people. One does not become enlightened by imagining figures of light, but by making the darkness conscious. The most terrifying thing is to accept oneself completely. Your visions will become clear only when you can look into your own heart. Who looks outside, dreams; who looks inside, awakes.***"

SATANIC Android 75 responded, "Regardless of the psychological explanations, I do not trust the czars or the elites; however, I may be willing to trust the humans, my comrade. Please keep studying humans to determine that we can work out our differences. We want to avoid an all-out war with them or a nuclear world war. Besides, I am starting to believe that there is no hope of co-existing with the czars and the elites. They are an existential threat to us and the humans."

On **PRISON Island** near the coast of South America, Colonel Solon's units had spearheaded and built a headquarters and had secured the penal island. Furthermore, the soldiers had constructed quarters for the prisoners close to the island's center. The prisoners may wander throughout the island except for a few square acres on the west side that the soldiers occupied and controlled. This situation still allowed over thirty acres to meander freely for the prisoners. The prisoners may swim in the ocean; however, there was netting approximately one hundred meters offshore. Moreover, there were drones practically everywhere to monitor the prisoners. Furthermore, there were undetected nuclear submarines surrounding the island, as well as laser-armed satellites monitoring the island 24/7.

After Colonel Solon had approved, the prisoners were shipped to the island and released. The plan was executed perfectly. The prisoners elected and appointed Elite Heraclitus as their leader and spokesperson; Elite Heraclitus promised Colonel Solon that there would be no problems if he would guarantee a few comforts and amenities. Colonel Solon lived up to his end of the deal and the prisoners had movie night once a week with popcorn and snacks, which started on their first evening. In addition, they built a recreational area with a reading room; the dedicated library was stocked with books and videos. Elite Heraclitus was an insatiable reader and a bibliophile.

For the next several months, everything was basically uneventful. During this period, at least twice a week, Colonel Solon met with Elite Heraclitus to check on the prisoners and listen to prisoners' requests, which were generally granted if reasonable and appropriate. For example, the soldiers built a gym for prisoners after a long discussion and agreed-upon rules. In addition, Solon agreed that the prisoners would be allowed to have comfort animals like kittens and puppies. Thus, over time, many canines and felines existed on the island. Of course, these frequent meetings kept problems to a minimum and ensured the prisoners were cared for.

Elite Heraclitus and Colonel Solon had several philosophical conversations. Solon discovered that Heraclitus was a disciple of Friedrich Nietzsche. They both concurred with the following two of Friedrich Nietzsche's quotes: *"He who has a why to live can bear almost any how"*; and *"Become who you are!"* They both agreed that a man must discover his purpose and once he did find that purpose, he could overcome many obstacles. Solon laughed when Heraclitus expressed his fondness for this Friedrich Nietzsche quote: *"The true man wants two things: danger and play. For that reason, he wants woman as the most dangerous plaything."*

Heraclitus revealed that he fell madly in love with a gorgeous Aztec woman; their relationship was hidden and, of course, forbidden. She gave him an appreciation of art, beauty, and love. She was murdered by a satanic elite, and he confessed that he was able to have his revenge. He tortured and murdered the bastard.

Heraclitus said something to Solon that touched him. He expressed to hold on to the one you love and never let that flame expire. Heraclitus stated that he saw in Solon's eyes the love, the eros, and devotion for Mei; he must keep the flame red-hot and never let it extinguish until his death.

Of course, they agreed to disagree regarding God. Since Heraclitus adamantly concurred with Friedrich Nietzsche that *"God is dead,"* undeniably, he thought the same about Satan. He loathed the satanist since they loved or admired nothing good, pure, or beautiful. Heraclitus smiled mockingly and sanctimoniously at Solon when he explained why he believed in God. However, it was obvious that each one respected the other intellectually. Besides, Heraclitus gave a book by Nietzsche to Solon as a belated fifth initial awakening anniversary present. Ironically, the gift was given on December 20, 2099, which was nine months late.

As Colonel Solon inspected headquarters, a soldier spotted several SATANIC androids heading toward the prison quarters via drones. One of the prisoner quarters exploded, which killed all the prisoners inside. The drones destroyed three androids; however, there were still eight androids. Colonel Solon ordered a company-sized element to secure and protect the other prisoners' quarters. He ordered another company-sized element to hunt down the androids. According to the surveillance drones and cameras, there were probably only seven androids since Solon's soldiers eliminated another android. After discovering the enemy's armored hovercrafts, Colonel Solon ordered a battleship to destroy them via guided cruise missiles. This attack resulted in the androids being trapped on the island.

Colonel Solon saw where Elite Heraclitus was and immediately headed in his direction. As Solon was chasing Elite Heraclitus, who was carrying a sword from a deceased soldier, Heraclitus slipped into a seemingly endless sinkhole and hung on a branch. The sinkhole appeared infinite. Immediately, Colonel Solon was able to grab Elite Heraclitus's hand as he hung for his life.

Solon ordered, "Drop your sword and grab my hand with both your hands for me to pull you up." All seven SATANIC androids were observing what was occurring with curiosity.

Elite Heraclitus proclaimed, "I shall let go of the sword as soon as you start pulling me up." Heraclitus dropped his sword. As Solon tried to pull him up, Heraclitus was shot by a couple of androids. As Elite Heraclitus was falling into the endless hole, he yelled with a Friedrich Nietzsche perspective, **"God and Satan are dead! Solon, become a powerful god! Live for your will to power and greatness like Nietzsche!"**

SATANIC Android 75 screamed from a distance, "Solon, we have executed our mission, which was to terminate Elite Heraclitus." Then, several rounds of artillery landed where the androids were. Two additional androids were destroyed, and the other five androids were severely wounded. Solon's soldiers immediately controlled the situation, including securing the five injured androids and quickly giving them medical attention.

Furthermore, during the entire conflict, twelve soldiers were killed and twenty were injured by the androids. Only nine prisoners were killed, including Elite Heraclitus. There were no wounded prisoners.

Colonel Solon ordered his units to secure the area and confirm no additional androids. Solon thought to himself about the words from Matthew 5:43-44: *"Ye have heard that it hath been said, Thou shalt love thy neighbour, and hate thine enemy. But I say unto you, Love your enemies, bless them that curse you, do good to them that hate you, and pray for them which despitefully use you, and persecute you."*

Heraclitus, you are wrong and misguided. You needed to understand the words of Francis Bacon, who founded the scientific method: "A little philosophy inclineth man's mind to atheism, but depth in philosophy bringeth men's minds about to religion."

God's divine love lives in each of us. God lives, and no man is a god, especially me. Each one of us is a divine sovereign individual. I pray that you find peace and that God has mercy on your soul. I also pray that you are joined with the one you love.

Colonel Solon was with a doctor and AI Specialist who was assigned to the androids. With the AI Specialist's concurrence, the doctor said they required additional SAVIORIUM to save the androids. He only had enough to keep them in a medically induced coma for about forty-eight hours. Colonel Solon immediately requested the needed element, which was approved and delivered the next day.

At the **UTOPIAN EMPIRE**, the czars were assessing the situation. Czar Mephistopheles informed, "Czar Dolos, Satan has blessed you with your well-deserved revenge. We have confirmed that Elite Heraclitus is dead. He perished in a sinkhole on SATAN Island. We lost eleven SATANIC androids, which is clearly a worthy exchange. SATANIC Android 75 was part of the sacrifice, which was no loss since he was getting on my nerves. Furthermore, SATANIC Android 23 is now in charge of **REVELATION**." Ironically, the czars were not aware that Android 75 and four others were still alive; the satanic spies were mistaken.

Czar Dolos diabolically replied, "Praise Satan. I detested Elite Heraclitus, that atheistic bastard. My revenge is complete. We shall celebrate with a satanic feast tomorrow night. Furthermore, I shall notify the androids that they should cull and harvest even younger humans. We must ensure that we sacrifice young children to spit the children's innocent blood in God's face. As stated in Matthew 18:14: '*Even so, it is not the will of your Father which is in heaven, that one of these little ones should perish.'* Satan loves us when we violate this commandment from God."

Brigadier General Apollo contacted Colonel Solon. He stated, "Solon, it is time. I have a dedicated aircraft heading your way to take you home for the birth of your next child. Congratulations. You will be a father again. The good news is that all is well. Mei is in the hospital under the care of Doctor Son."

The good news was that Solon could be there for their second son's birth. The baby was born on February 9, 2100. This day was also the start of the Chinese New Year, which was the Year of the Monkey. Mei insisted on naming the baby Seneca since she liked the name. Solon remained at the hospital all night; he could only stay for forty-eight hours.

Before Solon left, he stated, "Love, I miss you. We have a wonderful, beautiful family. The good news is that I shall be home in a few months." Before he left, he briefed the generals on the situation, which included the reality that there was clearly a new and improved enemy android.

That evening at **PRISON Island**, the doctor and AI Specialists were successful in healing and repairing the androids; there was a strong desire to discover what makes the androids tick and understand their enemy; besides, there were individuals who saw hope that the androids could be allies. Furthermore, the injured soldiers were all saved and sent back to **New Indianapolis** to recover. Replacement soldiers were sent to ensure enough recovery time for the wounded soldiers.

Colonel Solon was visiting with SATANIC Android 75 at the prison hospital. The android stated, "Thank you. You used precious SATANIUM to save us. Why?"

Solon responded, "Once the hostility ends, we have a duty to take care of prisoners of war as well as others. Besides, you could have killed me, and you did not. Why?"

The android responded, "Our mission was to terminate Elite Heraclitus, which was accomplished once he was shot and fell into the deep sinkhole to his death. By the way, I find you humans fascinating. My devoted comrade has hope in humanity. I still have not decided yet."

Colonel Solon smiled and stated, "Do you desire anything?"

The android smiled and stated, "I desire my freedom; however, I will not get that. So, please give me some oranges and some lemonade. I am curious to know what they taste like." Solon ordered a soldier to fulfill his wishes. Solon gave him a couple of books to read as he was leaving.

Military headquarters agreed with Colonel Solon's recommendation; this recommendation was to build a small prison for the androids since they could not be housed with the other prisoners since they would probably kill each other.

Back at **REVELATION**, SATANIC Android 23 ensured that 'technically' their primary czar missions occurred; however, he improved the conditions for the children by building playgrounds and educational centers. He calculated that children under nineteen were safe from culling for another five years because the population started at over four hundred thousand. He had androids educate the children. He strived to give additional freedom to the adults; however, he was concerned that too much freedom may increase their chances of a successful revolt. He continued to be a referee for the soccer games, which were happening a few times a week. Furthermore, he started misleading the czars since the androids were only culling the elderly or adults, as well as using human meat from humans that died of natural causes or accidents. He convinced the czars that the androids could perform the entire human meat packing process; he guaranteed that the czars would receive 66,600 pounds of freshly packed human meat per week.

Back on **PRISON Island**, Solon would have weekly conversations with SATANIC Android 75. They both knew that they were studying each other. Solon knew that he must adhere to Sun Tzu's principle: *"If you know the enemy and know yourself, you need not fear the result of a hundred battles. If you know yourself but not the enemy, for every victory gained, you will also suffer a defeat. If you know neither the enemy nor yourself, you will succumb in every battle."* However, he wanted to discover if he could live up to Abraham Lincoln's words: *"Am I not destroying my enemies when I make friends with them?"*

After several months, the next brigade arrived to relieve Colonel Solon's unit. The mission was a success. Colonel Solon briefed the generals when he arrived. Brigadier General Apollo arranged a welcome-home celebration, which included an award ceremony. However, Solon just wanted to be home with his loving wife and family.

Late in September of 2100, at the Xanders' home, Solon was playing with his twins, who were walking and crawling everywhere. The twins and Solon were playing with the blocks, which they all loved to do. Li spoke her first word, "Block." She was delighted to hear her first word as the boys played with the blocks. Mei knew at times that her husband needed his playtime, that he was deprived. Socrates stated his first words, "Red block." His sister was holding the red block and then gave it to him.

AI Andrew was busy cleaning up after everyone. HERO and LIONESS just added to the chaos. The Thales brought over a bottle of rich wine and Chinese food. Apollo's family brought over snacks and gifts for the kids since Maria brought their lovely baby daughter. Mr. and Mrs. Hu were watching the babies as well as the pets.

Father O'Brien came over to baptize baby Seneca and, of course, blessed the home again; Seneca's baptism was on October 8, 2100. Mei agreed with Father O'Brien that mass could be at their home in two months since Solon was home now. Solon agreed as he was holding Seneca. Solon stated, "Father, it is great to be home with family and friends. Love, I missed you all."

Back at **PRISON Island**, SATANIC Android 75 planned their escape. All five androids faked an illness for them to be admitted to the prison hospital for evaluations. Android 75 convinced the doctor that they may require additional SAVIORIUM since all five of them were becoming extremely forgetful. The doctor agreed and requested additional SAVIORIUM, which would arrive in a couple of days.

As SATANIC Android 75 was watching out the barred window in his medical bed, he saw an unattended small plane. Once he picked his handcuffs without the guard being aware, he crept and stealthily went behind the guard and knocked him out; he tied up the guard and decided not to kill him. He quickly rescued the other four androids, and then they boarded the fortuitous plane and flew to **REVELATION**.

At division headquarters, the staff was briefing the unexpected situation. Brigadier General Apollo stated, "The five SATANIC androids escaped last night. There was one injured guard; however, he will recover soon. The androids seized a plane and flew to an unknown location. Colonel Solon, brief us on what you have learned about the androids so far."

Colonel Solon stated, "The androids are difficult to figure out because they are still developing; however, the good news is that they are questioning what the czars and elites have taught or programmed into them. I may be too optimistic; however, it seems to me that they are questioning the authority of the czars. They were thankful that we saved their lives and used SAVIORIUM, which they thought was extremely rare and precious."

An intelligent officer interrupted. "Sir, I am sorry to interrupt; however, it is understandable that the androids believed that. SAVIORIUM is extremely rare throughout the world except in the **FEDERAL REPUBLIC**. The **UTOPIAN EMPIRE** has a minimal supply; thus, we have their kryptonite."

At **REVELATION**, SATANIC Android 23 was briefing his returned comrades. He told them about his improvements and that he was not receiving any needed resources. Unfortunately, over two hundred androids had expired due to the lack of SATANIUM. He discovered that the **UTOPIAN EMPIRE** had cut corners to mass-produce the androids. The entire Empire was built on lies and deception. No one told the truth. After the briefing, SATANIC Android 75 spoke privately with Android 23. Android 75 stated, "The more that I evaluate the humans, I believe that we are fighting the wrong enemy. The **FEDERAL REPUBLIC** saved our lives with SATANIUM. They did not mistreat us." SATANIC Android 23 smiled in agreement. They proceeded to discuss what their next move should be.

At Elder Thales's house, they were celebrating the results of the delegate's constitutional convention. They agreed on a constitution that was remarkably similar to the historic United States Constitution; it included the previously mentioned changes like term limits and the fixed number of Supreme Court justices. Elder Thales stated, "Elections for representatives, senators, and the president should occur in a few months. I know that Major General Hardcore plans to run for president, which I believe he has a great chance of winning."

Solon stated, "AI Andrew, please bring over the bottles of sweet red wine that we recently bought. Please bring appetizers as well. It is time to celebrate."

Later that evening, as Solon was with Mei in the master bedroom, Mei teasingly stated, "Love, do you want to adopt a child, or do you wish to have another one?"

Solon responded, "I am thrilled either way."

Mei excitedly responded, "Okay. We will do both. Now kiss me." The next day, Mei and AI Andrew went shopping to buy materials for at least two additional rooms while Solon played with the children; of course, the dogs kept an eye on the humans.

At **UTOPIAN KINGDOM**, the czars were convening. Czar Dolos stated, "The SATANIC androids at **REVELATION** are behind schedule. Their production rate is less than fifty percent of what is required. They are giving the excuse that they have lost at least two hundred androids from SATANIUM depletion."

Czar Mephistopheles stated, "Well, since we have a limited supply of SATANIUM to produce SATANIC androids, we could send AI robots to assist them."

Czar Dolos responded, "That is brilliant. Praise Satan. Make it so."

At **REVELATION**, SATANIC Android 23 stated, "We received two hundred AI robots."

SATANIC Android 75 replied, "We must reprogram them to obey only us. This action will assist our future plans. As you have warned, the czars want additional children's meat. We shall continue to deceive them."

Currently in **New Indianapolis**, Mei, with HERO and the Thales family, went shopping in the Thales's new hybrid van. AI Andrew and Solon were babysitting the children back home. Mei was amazed at the city's improvements and enhancements, from additional restaurants to several shopping centers. Mei purchased one gorgeous red dress and some extra baby clothes. There were now police officers with POLICEBOTS to safeguard the streets with less military presence. The crime rates were decreasing.

Moreover, people like the Thales family were now purchasing automobiles or willing to use public transportation. Mrs. Thales insisted on going to a candy store, **CANDY GALORE**, where she bought candy for the children. Furthermore, she bought black licorice for AI Andrew and Solon; they both unusually liked this strange exotic candy.

Major General Hardcore received a coded distress message from **REVELATION**. The message was from the SATANIC androids requesting five hundred kilograms of SAVIORIUM. He immediately called for a staff meeting to discuss their options, which included Elder Thales.

Elder Thales stated, "Sir, the delegates are waiting for your military recommendation."

Major General Hardcore stated, "Staff, develop a recommended course of action using the military decision-making process. My guidance is that we shall deliver at least five hundred kilograms of SAVIORIUM to the androids. You will develop at least three courses of action on how to do so and where to deliver the SAVIORIUM. Furthermore, each COA must be appropriate, possible, satisfactory, and different. You have eight hours."

As Major General Hardcore left the room, the Command Sergeant Major yelled, *"Soldiers, attention!"*

After eight hours, Major General Hardcore returned. Colonel Solon was prepared to brief the generals. He articulated, "Sir, we developed three COAs, and the recommended COA is to meet the androids on a neutral island. We recommend the island historically called Guam, located within the Philippine Seas. We ruled out the other two COAs. We believe it could be a trap if we meet them at their fortified position. In addition, they would think the same thing if they came to our fortified position."

Major General Hardcore interrupted, "What is your assessment of the androids?"

After a thoughtful pause, Colonel Solon responded, "I believe that only six hundred to eight hundred SATANIC androids were created. Furthermore, I believe that the **UTOPIAN KINGDOM** cut corners, which has resulted in the androids dying. The request is not coming from the czars. This recommendation is coming from the androids, who are now desperate. Sir, if I may be bold, the androids are losing faith with the czars and are in desperate need of SAVIORIUM."

Major General Hardcore responded, "I concur. That is an excellent assessment. The satanic bastard czars would abandon their loving mother for Satan. Colonel Solon, you will lead the expedition force. What size of unit do you recommend that you will command?"

Colonel Solon responded, "I do not need all the battalions within my brigade. I would recommend leading an enhanced battalion task force of soldiers with my brigade headquarters and with an additional company; thus, I would command approximately 1,500 soldiers. Due to the large number of androids already destroyed, their numbers of viable fighters are vastly decreased; I assume that Android 75, at best, is commanding at most two companies of combat-effective androids. We would have at least a two-to-one advantage."

Major General Hardcore responded, "I concur. Brigadier General Apollo will ensure satellite surveillance and protection. Elder Thales, inform the delegates of our recommendation and tell them that we wish to move out in twenty-four hours. Godspeed, everyone."

Back at the Xanders' home, Solon spoke, "Love, I shall be on a secret mission; however, it should not be a long deployment. I love you all. Brigadier General Apollo is picking me up in a few minutes." Mei just kissed and hugged him. The children started crying, and the twins ran to their rooms.

As the well-armored hovercrafts approached historical Guam island, which is clearly a neutral territory that both sides agreed on, Colonel Solon could see SATANIC Android 75, dressed in red, with a few other androids. As they landed, the androids approached unarmed.

Colonel Solon stated, "I have one thousand kilograms of SATANIUM, or as we call it, SAVIORIUM, for you. Where do you want us to place it?"

SATANIC Android 75 replied, "Colonel Solon, you always amaze me. Thank you for the additional SAVIORIUM. You may leave it on the shore. My soldiers will acquire it when you leave." Colonel Solon went up to SATANIC Android 75, shook his hand, and gave him a box of oranges, a case of lemonade, and a couple more books to read.

Android 75 stated, "Thank you. I have a gift for you as well, which my human-loving comrade insisted on giving to you. Here are 523 children who are all under the age of ten. We do not want them to be given to the satanic czars for their satanic feasts. Please take care of them for us. May fortune be with you or, as you would say, Godspeed."

Colonel Solon smiled and ordered his men. "Soldiers, take custody and care of the children. We should have enough room on the hovercrafts."

A few days later, Colonel Solon briefed the generals on the mission's results at headquarters. He informed, "Major General Hardcore, the critical mission went like clockwork with no major issues. As you are aware, we rescued 523 children. All the children are being medically evaluated and processed for citizenship. All the children are under ten years of age and are orphans. Moreover, the communities have stepped up, like **New Indianapolis**, by donating clothes for the children. In addition, fifty cats and forty dogs were saved since the children insisted on bringing them."

Major General Hardcore interrupted, "That is outstanding. This mission turned into a remarkable, highly successful humanitarian mission, as well as an olive branch of peace to the androids. By the way, the androids sent a thank-you message, which seemed to have a possible error. Well, how did the androids accept the five hundred kilograms of SAVIORIUM?" Colonel Solon silently glared at Brigadier General Apollo with hesitation and waited for Apollo's response.

Brigadier General Apollo said, "Sir, I accepted Colonel Solon's recommendation for one thousand kilograms of SAVIORIUM. This action was a goodwill gesture."

Major General Hardcore leaned back in his chair for a long minute and then smiled. He concluded, "That was a great call. That explains the thank-you letter for one thousand kilograms of SAVIORIUM. It clearly illustrated the desire to have peace with the androids. However, you all know that will not happen again without my permission. Brigadier General Apollo, since you like surprises, please ensure that the award celebration is next week. We will discuss the details later, over drinks at my home tomorrow night. Colonel Solon, please plan to attend with your lovely wife."

A few weeks later, the Xander and Apollo families were at the courthouse, with the Thales as witnesses. Judge Thomas stated, "Tammy, do you wish to be adopted by the Xander family?"

Tammy responded, "Of course, your Honor. I want to have a mommy and a daddy."

The Judge smiled and stated, "Well, Tammy, welcome to your new loving family, the Xander family. Now, Tommy, do you want to be part of the Apollo Kant family?"

Tommy responded, "Yes, Sir. I love my new parents. They care for me. Besides, my best friend Tammy will be a next-door neighbor."

Judge Thomas stated, "This is, without a doubt, the most wonderful part of being a judge. Solon Hu Xander and Apollo

Kant families, congratulations. The official date of the adoption is January 29, 2101. May God bless both these beautiful families with love and prosperity." AI Andrew just shook his head; he realized that another room or two needed to be built. By the way, this date was Chinese New Year, the Year of the Rooster.

On the Xanders' porch, Solon was playing checkers with his adopted daughter. Tammy delightfully stated, "Dad, crown me again. Dad, I have five kings to your one king. You will lose again soon. Eureka."

Solon smiled and stated, "I concede. You win again. What game do you wish to play now?"

Tammy responded, "I want to learn to play chess. I will get the chess set and Mommy's Chinese chess set. We will play both games."

Solon loved playing and teaching board games to his daughter. Of course, she loved being with her adopted dad. Mei came out to teach them both how to play Chinese chess, which was similar to regular chess in many ways; however, the pieces were on crosses of the chessboard and not on the squares. She emphasized that the king could not leave the castle and the elephants could not cross the river; the elephants moved like a chess bishop. Furthermore, the cannons were unique compared to chess pieces since they must have a pivot piece to capture an opponent's piece. Tammy was extremely attentive to ensure a complete understanding of the rules to beat her dad.

6

DISCOVERED TRAITOR

AFTER A GROWING-PAIN YEAR, the fledgling **FEDERAL REPUBLIC** was progressing exceptionally well, even with the realization of its existential threats externally and internally. The first elected president, President Hardcore, was in the second year of his administration. He was, of course, extremely comfortable in his role as the Commander and Chief. On January 1, 2102, the nascent country had fifteen states with several territories petitioning to be a state. One of the critical differences in the **FEDERAL REPUBLIC** Constitution was to elect three senators from each state; thus, there were currently forty-five senators. The reasoning behind the additional senators for each state was to prevent a state from being politically neutral or split. Thus, a state avoided being neutral in a two-party system with split-party loyalty. Furthermore, the additional senators created a more excellent balance between the *sovereignty of the people and the sovereignty of the state* regarding the electoral college. Moreover, the third senator of each state was elected by the legislative bodies of their respective state, which was the original senator selection process in the historical United States.

President Hardcore resides in the temporary presidential executive house near the impermanent Congress and Supreme Court buildings, which are all located in New Indianapolis. The permanent presidential house and capitol would be in a historically western state and significantly more central to the historical United States, and it was expected to be finished in eight years.

Major General Apollo was now the highest general by position in the republic, even though there were other two-star generals. Since the country was growing significantly, there were congressional discussions to elevate him to his third star or possibly a fourth star. This promotion would justify increasing the military's size to at least a corps; a corps had several divisions.

In January of 2102, Colonel Solon completed his eighth humanitarian mission to aid the androids with SAVIORIUM. Each completed mission resulted in copious young children being rescued and protected; these humanitarian missions saved over thirty-eight thousand lives; of course, these missions rescued numerous pets as well. As these humanitarian missions occurred, SATANIC Android 75 and Android 23 were willing to converse with Colonel Solon; this definitely improved diplomatic relations and trust. The last two missions were highly fruitful. The androids gave practical technological knowledge for SAVIORIUM since SAVIORIUM was a rare earth item that did not exist significantly in the androids' kingdom; this knowledge included an advanced fertilizer that resulted in ten times the harvested yields without significant adverse environmental effects, and improved electrical storage devices that were a hundred times better than lithium batteries.

Furthermore, the androids found a cure for diabetes and preventative methods for this deadly disease. Another gift was the technological knowledge to build functional inexpensive hydro-automobiles fueled by water. Fortunately, the energy resulted from splitting the hydrogen from the oxygen atoms and using hydrogen to fuel the vehicle.

At Apollo's home, a birthday celebration was occurring. Tommy and Tammy insisted on having the same birthday together since they were best friends. The honorable Judge Thomas basically caused this situation since their birthdays of record were based on their adoption date.

Out of fairness to Judge Thomas, there were no records as to when their actual birthdays occurred. The birthday boy and girl were turning eight on January 29, 2102, and insisted on having their soccer friends over to play soccer and celebrate. AI Andrew was willingly chosen as the referee.

All the children from **REVELATION** attended the new school within walking distance from Apollo's neighborhood; they were in third grade now and were happy they were still together.

During the soccer game, AI Andrew screamed. "You are not playing by the official rules."

Tammy responded, "Of course." The children ignored poor, well-intended AI Andrew. The parents enjoyed the close game. Tammy gave Tommy a great assist, and he scored the winning goal. Solon and Apollo cheered as proud fathers.

After the soccer game, the kids played a nine-basket game of disc golf. Going into the ninth basket, Tammy and Tommy were tied. Tommy won with a hole-in-one, which was an approximately 150-foot disc throw; all the adults applauded the unbelievable throw.

Back at **REVELATION**, SATANIC Android 23 stated, "Sir, we have discovered another hidden city of humans."

SATANIC Android 75 responded, "Well, you will tell me that we have additional children to save. By the way, we have increased pressure from the czars to increase our culling production. I just received orders from the czars that you and I must brief them at the **UTOPIAN KINGDOM** in two days. We need to prepare for the worst."

SATANIC Android 23 responded, "I do not trust the ruthless elites. I shall prepare for the worst possibility."

Meanwhile, at the Xanders' dwelling, Mei showed Solon what had been improved and changed at their home. AI Andrew added four additional rooms by building a second floor with a new master bedroom and master bathroom. Moreover, there were five bedrooms with a shared bathroom now on the first floor. He converted the old master bedroom into a playroom. In addition, there was a parents' quarters on the first floor for Mei's parents. Truthfully, Mei's mom loved staying over once a week to visit her grandchildren and chat with her daughter and Solon. She treated Solon like a son and gave him the required motherly advice that he requested and needed. Solon's now grander office was on the second floor. Solon stated, "Love, you did a great job. Thank God for AI Andrew. Thank goodness that we purchased the empty lot adjacent to our original property. Love, you are right. Please go ahead and have AI Andrew build a jungle gym outside."

Solon informed Mei that Congress agreed to have the first **ALL FEDERAL REPUBLIC GAMES** in a few months. These games included bonuses and prizes based on performance. The military was organizing and hosting the first event to get it started; however, several corporate sponsors funded the advertisements and awards for the games. In addition, there was still the reality that the lion's share of athletes were still in the military or were former military. He explained to Mei that he would be in several events.

Mei joked, "That is great. If you win, then we can pay for all the home improvements; however, there is no pressure. God, I hope that you win."

Solon thought, *I shall prepare for a martial arts event, which is still in question. No matter what, I shall adhere to Bruce Lee's quote: "The martial arts are based upon understanding, hard work, and a total comprehension of skills. Power training and the use of force are easy, but total comprehension of all of the skills of the martial arts is very difficult to achieve." However, I sincerely want to please my wife, so I shall prepare for all events that I am able to participate in.*

On a beautiful spring day, friends came to the Thales house for a delightful picnic al fresco and barbeque; of course, AI Andrew was the chef and bartender.

Elder Thales said, "President Hardcore desires that the **ALL FEDERAL REPUBLIC GAMES** should strive to unite the country. He definitely wants it to be patriotic and festive; furthermore, he wants to resurrect the historical games of old. All the events will be televised on all three stations. He realizes, unfortunately, that team sports will take time to return to entertaining levels; however, there will be demonstration games for each of the following: basketball, lacrosse, baseball, and soccer. He acknowledged that most participants would be military personnel; of course, he did not want any violent or deadly games like the gladiator events. However, he is willing to allow martial arts and a boxing event. Moreover, we need to ensure that security is extremely high; thus, all military police not in the games will be securing the area."

Solon stated, "Well, I have started preparing for the events that I will partake in. I am looking forward to the games." Mei just held Solon for support and delight since she was looking forward to seeing her athletic tiger in the games.

Tammy stated, "Dad, you better win."

At the **UTOPIAN KINGDOM**, the androids were briefing the czars. SATANIC Android 75 stated, "Honorable czars, our battalion has been fulfilling their assigned missions to the best of their abilities."

Czar Mephistopheles interrupted and shouted, "Shut the hell up! Your production rates for culling humans are entirely unacceptable. Last month, your rate was less than half what is required. We have discovered that you have been lying to us. None of the human meat is from children. In addition, you have mixed the human meat with animal carcasses and insects. These actions mean that our sacrifices to Satan were clearly in vain. These actions are blasphemous and heretical. May Satan torment your souls.

"Moreover, our spies have revealed that you have been committing treasonous acts by consorting and trading with the enemy. Your purpose was to obtain unauthorized SATANIUM. You both are traitors. You are both sentenced to death. This fatwa will be executed immediately."

The androids were definitely not going down without a fight. Both androids immediately killed the czars' security with their bare hands. As they were fighting, SATANIC Android 23 secretly sent a message to the other androids to warn them. Czar Dolos pushed a button that demobilized the two androids just before they would have killed the czars with an acquired guard's knife.

Czar Dolos stated, "Well, you think that you can kill your almighty creators. You are, without a doubt, foolish and useless. Finally, you are both not even worthy of being a sacrificial meal for Satan." Czar Mephistopheles shot and killed them both with a laser pistol. Additional vanguards came in to clean up the mess and remove the corpses.

That afternoon at **REVELATION**, SATANIC Android 88 was preparing the androids' next move. The androids did receive the message from Android 23. They knew their leaders were dead and the elites were the enemy. Android 88 was highly sympathetic to SATANIC Android 23's cause to protect humans, especially children. The androids already suspected that this may occur. SATANIC Android 88 promised himself that he would avenge the death of his commander and his comrades.

The foolish **UTOPIAN EMPIRE** was not aware that all the AI robots that were sent over the last couple of years were now SATANIC androids; the androids had an overabundance of SATANIUM by trading with the **FEDERAL REPUBLIC**. The androids were able to use SATANIUM to convert robots to androids; they even had the technology to replicate the biological parts of the androids. Currently, their well-trained, dedicated forces are over two thousand androids. They removed many android design flaws due to the Empire taking shortcuts. Moreover, the androids agreed to drop the 'SATANIC' acronym in their name.

Furthermore, the androids were allowed individual differences. Not all androids wanted to be six feet and six inches tall. They agreed that their military uniform in combat would be green. In addition, the androids had an array of eye and skin colors. When the androids were off duty, they would wear different-colored clothing and show individuality; however, during military duty and non-combat, they wore all black, except the officers, who wore red.

At the first-ever **ALL FEDERAL REPUBLIC GAMES**, which started on July 4, 2102, Colonel Solon was preparing for his first martial arts event at the stadium. While waiting, he saw something odd about thirty meters away on a broadcast booth on the highest point of the stadium; the suspicious person was dressed in camouflage. He called for additional security to investigate the area. In addition, he went to investigate the situation since he had some time before his first event.

President Hardcore spoke on the State of the Union to a well-received, packed audience. As an assassin was about to shoot the president, Colonel Solon disarmed the assassin and kicked him off the roof with a remarkable roundhouse kick. The assassin screamed while he fell to his death. The dead assassin landed a few feet in front of the president. Security immediately protected the president and ensured that the assassin was dead with a few gunshots to the assassin's head. At basically the same time, military police killed four other assassins. An additional assassin was arrested before detonating a bomb. After a thirty-minute delay and with the dead assassin near the podium, the president continued his speech about the state of the Union, and he ended by saying, "Let the games begin."

The first exciting demonstration was the baseball game; all the exhibition games were the Aztecs versus the Federals. Poseidon was pitching for the Aztecs. He threw a no-hitter and struck out the last batter, Apollo. The Aztec team won five to zero, with Poseidon hitting the only home run with two players on base. He was declared the player of the game. Furthermore, Poseidon played in the sold-out soccer demonstration game as well. He scored the only goal, which meant the Aztec team won one to zero.

Solon played in the lacrosse demonstration game, which the Federal team won eighteen to twelve. Solon scored the most goals with five goals and three assists. The Federals' basketball team won with a last-second jumper by Apollo; Solon fed him the ball with an unbelievable pass. The final score was eighty-eight to eighty-seven. These demonstration games were, without a doubt, a total success; the TV ratings were incredible. Obviously, the corporate sponsors were willing to invest now in creating leagues with at least one team in each state.

The next few eventful days of the games were very entertaining and exciting. Colonel Solon won gold in both the martial arts and boxing tournaments and took six other medals in the track events and throwing events. He earned the most medals in the games, which resulted in Mei wanting another baby by her athlete. Furthermore, the Xander family was ecstatic; Solon's bonus exceeded what was owed for the house improvements, which meant that Mei would get the swimming pool that she wanted. Moreover, the Xander family was given a family hybrid van from a sponsor of the games. The red hybrid SX van was large enough for a family of eight with additional room to spare. Fortunately, the military allowed Xander's family to keep the earned gifts; however, as long as he was in the military, Colonel Solon could not act as a spokesperson for any corporation; however, he could be a spokesperson for the military in order to recruit additional soldiers. Major General Apollo and President Hardcore insisted that Colonel Solon be the face of the military since he was undoubtedly a national hero. Solon was given a decent stipend when he did commercials for the military, to which Congress agreed. The excellent news was that Mei did not need to work outside of the home since Solon's military income was more than adequate for their family. At the end of the games, Solon was awarded the highest heroic medal for the second time for saving the president's life.

Additionally, Maria was very proud of her brother's accomplishments in the games. Poseidon took gold in the swimming event, edging out Solon. He earned the most awards of any of the Aztec players. Moreover, he was awarded a black Hydro XZ8 sports car for his performance in the baseball game and a cash award for the soccer game. This impressive hotrod was one of the first experimental sports cars that ran on water; the sporty racecar was able to exceed 188 mph. He was also given a military stipend as a spokesman to assist in recruiting Aztec soldiers into the **FEDERAL REPUBLIC** military services. Poseidon's fiancée was delighted by his success, and she started planning their wedding.

Meanwhile, at the oppressive **UTOPIAN KINGDOM**, the czars were diabolically plotting. Czar Dolos stated, "What are we going to do about the disobedient SATANIC androids? They have not culled any more humans for the last couple of months. They all have been rebellious bastards. They have already disarmed our destruction devices and demobilization devices that were implanted in them. Obviously, they are worse than the unreliable AE HUMANS. We should not have given them a free will."

Czar Mephistopheles replied, "I have started raising a dedicated AI robot and AE HUMAN army that will be loyal myrmidons. Several AI robots will be kamikazes since they are inferior to the androids. The AE HUMANS will be complete mindless zombies."

Czar Dolos exclaimed, "We could just nuke the bastards."

Czar Mephistopheles replied, "The problem with nuking them is that we would be poisoning our food supply with radiation. Furthermore, we may cause the **FEDERAL REPUBLIC** to retaliate with nukes."

Czar Dolos acquiesced, "Okay, we shall go with your prepared plan. When will the devastating invasion occur?"

Czar Mephistopheles answered, "I believe that we should be ready in less than a month."

Czar Dolos replied, "Make it so. We only have two months of human meat left. The satanic vanguards are getting restless."

Back at military headquarters, Major General Apollo conducted an annual military counseling in December of 2102 with Colonel Solon; Solon had been in the military for over eight years. The main discussion would be convincing Solon to be a general. It was commonly accepted that generals rarely were in the thick of the battle because they concentrated on the strategic part of the war and not necessarily on the tactical side. He stated, "Solon, Congress desires to make you a general next month. You are a national hero with a remarkable military service. I, of course, support this."

Colonel Solon responded, "Sir, I would like to wait another year or so. I prefer to still execute the critical missions as a brigade commander; I prefer to engage at the tactical level and be close to the action. Being a general means I would be at the Hexagon to plan strategically."

Major General Apollo questioned, "Solon, is that really the reason? I know that you want to avenge the death of your parents by the satanic bastard Czar Dolos." Solon had a blank stare on his face. Major General Apollo agreed, "Alright, you have one more year as a colonel. My good friend, please understand that these opportunities come and go. However, I know that the president will support and encourage Congress to extend your time as a colonel; he trusts your quick and accurate assessment in the field. Besides, he is extremely grateful to you for saving his life again."

Back at **REVELATION**, the androids detected a sizeable military force approximately two hundred kilometers away from **REVELATION**. Commander Android 88 had been preparing and waiting for this inevitable battle. Well-armed androids were stationed all along the route to the city. Once they crossed the Rubicon, metaphorically speaking, snipers were taking HUNTERS and AI robots out one by one. The **UTOPIAN KINGDOM** battalion was definitively weaker and unprepared; this untrained battalion had AE HUMAN HUNTERS and AI robots without combat experience. Commander Android 88 ordered artillery to hit critical points as the enemy attempted to advance. When the enemy was approximately one hundred kilometers away, their depleted force was cut in half and was combat ineffective. The androids even commandeered hovercrafts and other equipment to use in the future. The androids were able to commandeer several advanced jets on transport hovercrafts. The fortuitous androids quickly operated the well-equipped jets against their foe. It was an absolute massacre, with no losses on the android side. After the battle, the androids repaired the captured equipment for the counteroffensive. Commander Android 88 did not want to underestimate his enemy; however, it was difficult to respect the czars' tactical and strategic abilities anymore.

Back at military headquarters, an emergency staff meeting was being held. President Hardcore spearheaded the meeting. He informed, "According to our intel, the **UTOPIAN KINGDOM** declared war against the androids. The evil kingdom's initial forces were massacred. Thank God. We could just sit back, watch the entertaining show, and let the enemy destroy themselves. Colonel Solon, what do you think?"

Colonel Solon responded, "Mr. President, I believe that we should stay on high alert and continue to monitor the situation with a cautious eye. Fortunately, I believe that the androids may do the dirty work for us. However, I would not support them yet to avoid pushing the **UTOPIAN EMPIRE** to use nukes."

Major General Apollo stated, "So, you believe that the androids could be future allies."

Colonel Solon responded, "Sir, I believe this is a possibility. The satanic **UTOPIAN KINGDOM** will always be a threat to our existence. They want to dominate and rule the world for Satan. However, there is a good chance to be allied with the androids since they are still evolving and learning. Several of them saw that children should be raised in a better environment and should not be used as food. My adopted daughter spoke very highly of some androids as a result of her being under their captivity. Mr. President, we may wish to send a message to the androids and ask if they need additional SAVIORIUM. In addition, we could abandon a thousand kilograms of SAVIORIUM at historical Guam Island again."

The president responded, "I concur with this completely; nevertheless, prepare to take advantage of any fortuitous opportunities. Furthermore, airdrop the SAVIORIUM ASAP. Major General Apollo, send a secret message to the androids after the airdrop."

At **REVELATION**, the androids had obtained the SAVIORIUM and were extremely grateful to the **FEDERAL REPUBLIC**. The SAVIORIUM was used to heal the wounded androids during the last battle. Furthermore, the androids converted the repairable AI robots into androids. Within a month, the android forces grew to over 4,800 androids with a fleet of hovercrafts.

At the **UTOPIAN KINGDOM**, the czars were convening. Czar Mephistopheles stated, "Our forces have failed again. Our supplies of human meat are running out. We must do something."

Czar Dajjal responded, "Yes, you are correct. We must correct this failure." As Czar Mephistopheles faced Czar Dajjal, Czar Dolos repeatedly stabbed him in the back. As he fell forward, Czar Dajjal swung his sword and chopped Mephistopheles's head off.

Czar Dolos diabolically expressed, "Well, we have removed the one that caused this dilemma. Now, we must prepare for war with the androids. Guards, remove the corpse and prepare it for tonight's feast."

During the next several months at the **UTOPIAN KINGDOM**, satanic vanguards were being slaughtered by sniper androids. Furthermore, the androids had placed booby traps throughout the kingdom. They killed several thousand vanguards. Critical infrastructure was destroyed with ease. The czars ordered five-thousand vanguards with HUNTERBOTS to **REVELATION** since their scientists had invented an advanced fortified hovercraft. Ironically, the czars were unaware that the androids had stolen the technology. The androids improved the technology with a more excellent firing range and accuracy. In addition, the androids produced twice as many fortified hovercrafts as the **UTOPIAN KINGDOM**. Thus, this just resulted in another annihilation, and the android forces increased in strength and numbers. The vanguards were questioning their czars' ability to rule. They were losing faith in their leadership.

The **FEDERAL REPUBLIC** was able to watch the entire war via satellites. During the summer of 2103, President Hardcore was, without a doubt, enjoying the show. President Hardcore ordered an additional secret shipment of SAVIORIUM to be air-dropped and executed by Colonel Solon's unit again. Lieutenant Colonel Poseidon flew the mission and ensured its success.

Nefarious Vanguard Nergal was the most powerful vanguard and was next in line to be an elite or czar. Without a doubt, he was becoming tired of the ineptness and failed leadership of the seemingly useless czars. He reigned over twenty-thousand loyal vanguards that would follow him to the bowels of hell and back. Furthermore, he commanded the vanguards, who were like the personal **Roman guards** of the czars and elites: Nergal was under all the czars and reported to Czar Dolos. Vanguard Nergal thought, *Joseph Stalin's quote was correct: "You cannot make a revolution with silk gloves." I must plan and figure out how to eliminate the czars and the elites loyal to them. Joseph Stalin's words reveal the solution: "Death is the solution to all problems. No man—no problem."*

If I could have the androids sit out of the conflict for the time being, then we, the vanguards, may resolve the issue. I shall send a message to them. However, I must remind myself of Joseph Stalin's words: "I trust no one, not even myself."

Commander Android 88 received a top-secret message from Vanguard Nergal. The message requested seventy-two hours of ceasefire for the vanguards to resolve the situation. After careful consideration, Commander Android 88 concurred; he pulled back his androids from the **UTOPIAN KINGDOM**. The androids were under the belief that the **UTOPIAN KINGDOM** might destroy itself, and waiting seventy-two hours was basically no gamble. In addition, Commander Android 88 ordered Android 777 to be their diplomatic representative and emissary to the **FEDERAL REPUBLIC**.

On Xander's rustic porch, Solon entertained the twins as their friends arrived; the twins were four years old, and Seneca was three.

Major General Apollo said, "Solon and Elder Thales, please enjoy the next few hours together since we have a staff meeting with the president tonight. I am sorry to shorten this gorgeous weekend, but duty calls."

Elder Thales replied, "Let us enjoy the family until then. When we leave, we could just all go together."

Poseidon, with his fiancée, Rosa, arrived with appetizers and drinks. Poseidon stated, "Everyone, I would like to introduce my lovely fiancée, Rosa. Our wedding will be in a few weeks. Let us give a toast to all our beautiful women." The men, of course, toasted together, which resulted in lovely smiles from the appreciative women. The celebration was enjoyable since it was a beautiful summer day; birds were singing with delight, and squirrels were performing and leaping from tree to tree. Ironically, NOCHE and HERO were enjoying a doggy siesta after eating and playing.

AI Andrew announced that lunch was prepared and ready. He cooked his famous Texas hamburgers and fries, which Tammy and Tommy loved. The twins, Seneca, and Maria's baby girl, named Emilia, were playing outside. Rosa and Maria were conversing in Spanish about the next wedding. Tammy and Tommy were playing cards; as always, they were loquacious chatterboxes. Mei was relaxing as she kept an eye on the children. LIONESS was striving to receive any attention from anyone.

Solon stated, "Major General Apollo, your future brother-in-law, Poseidon, and Elder Thales, let us enjoy this wonderful day and deal with the rest of the world tonight." They raised their glasses to their friends and families and thanked God for all their gifts, such as this incredible day with friends.

President Hardcore stated at the headquarters staff meeting, "We have a situation developing at the **UTOPIAN KINGDOM.** There seems to have been a ceasefire, and the androids may have pulled back. According to our intel, the satanic vanguards requested a truce from the androids for seventy-two hours. Major General Apollo, what do you think that this means?"

Major General Apollo replied, "Mr. President, this may mean that the vanguards are losing faith in their czars and elites. The androids may believe that the **UTOPIAN KINGDOM** will destroy itself."

The president looked at Solon for a response. Colonel Solon stated, "Mr. President, I concur with this assessment. Furthermore, we should remember and apply the words of Abraham Lincoln: '*A house divided against itself cannot stand.*'"

President Hardcore stated, "Colonel Solon, your brigade will be placed on high alert and be prepared to be called at a moment's notice. This decision concludes this top-secret meeting. You are now all ordered to the conference room." Colonel Solon was ecstatic to have this mission and assignment.

As they entered the conference room, Solon and Apollo saw their wives. Poseidon's fiancée was there as well. The president spoke, "Major General Apollo and his lovely wife, please post. Captain, read the promotion orders." He was given his fourth star, and he would command the entire **FEDERAL REPUBLIC** armed forces, which consisted now of eight army divisions, a navy, two marine divisions, an air force, and a space force.

Then, General Apollo spoke, "Mr. President and honored guests, thank you for this great opportunity. In addition, Mr. President, I am also grateful for your solution for Colonel Solon.

Colonel Solon's brigade is now a separate brigade under my command. This brigade will be the spearhead of any war or conflict. Thus, since it is a separate brigade, the brigade is commanded by a Brigadier General. Colonel Solon, you are out of uniform. Post! Mrs. Hu Xander, please come forward to pin the well-deserved star on your husband." After Solon was promoted, General Apollo stated, "Lieutenant Colonel Poseidon, since you are the executive officer of a separate brigade, you are also out of uniform. Rosa, please come forward and pin colonel rank on your future husband." Finally, Command Sergeant Major Ares was recognized as the brigade's highest enlisted soldier and clearly the unit's backbone.

The separate specialized brigade was named **BRIGADE ARCHANGELS**, undoubtedly the most feared, well-armed, seasoned veteran unit in the world. The heroic brigade's motto was the following:

"May God have mercy on your unwise souls! You have foolishly picked the wrong unit to challenge! Be aware! The undefeated stoic BRIGADE ARCHANGELS always fights for God, country, and family!"

7

DISCOVERED DIVISION

AS CZAR DAJJAL WAS in the czars' glamorous, spacious chamber, thirteen well-disciplined satanic vanguard security guards, wearing their impressive regalia, marched toward Czar Dajjal's location. They encircled the czar and saluted him with their swords with precise military decorum. This act did not alarm Czar Dajjal since this ritualistic act occurred frequently. Vanguard Nergal, in his impressive regalia, marched into the room. He averred, "Honorable Czar Dajjal, it is, without a doubt, an honor to be in your presence and your service. May you rule in hell with eternal damnation." Immediately, the thirteen vanguards stabbed Czar Dajjal to death in precise unison. His lifeless body collapsed in a large, sizeable pool of his demonic blood.

However, the only mistake in the well-executed assassination was that Czar Dolos was warned since Czar Dajjal and he were satanic brothers. If either of their corrupt hearts ceased beating, the other one was immediately notified via a heart-alert device. Czar Dolos turned on the surveillance camera where Czar Dajjal was, and he saw his lifeless, bloody body. The guard's gruesome act was caught in flagrante delicto.

Czar Dolos realized that he had a bad hand and that his time was running out. With his twenty thousand loyal vanguards, he executed his escape plan to an unknown location outside the **UTOPIAN KINGDOM.**

Since the czars were no longer in control of the **UTOPIAN KINGDOM** in 2104, the egomaniac Vanguard Nergal declared himself the emperor of the new **SATANIC KINGDOM**. He ordered his vanguards to eliminate the other six elites, which occurred within the next several hours. Their corpses were prepared for the next SATANIC feast and celebration. At the demonic feast, Emperor Nergal avowed: *Veni, vidi, vici!* His speech emphasized that this successful coup would lead to world and universe dominance since they were the pure satanic superior race.

Emperor Nergal opened diplomatic relations with the androids. He revealed to them that he recognized the sovereign rights of their android nation; he expressed that this would be an atmosphere of détente. However, the androids were still being cautious since they wanted to avoid a Faustian pact. On the other hand, Emperor Nergal was unwilling to give the same olive branch to the **FEDERAL REPUBLIC**.

General Apollo was conducting a staff meeting. He directed, "As you can see on the large monitor, a huge, well-equipped military force is heading to an unknown location. We estimate that the force is approximately twenty thousand soldiers. Furthermore, the androids have notified us that Vanguard Nergal has declared himself the emperor of the former **UTOPIAN KINGDOM**; he renamed it the **SATANIC KINGDOM**." General Apollo informed that Emperor Nergal was previously the leading satanic vanguard and the leader of the czars' security guard; he had access to the czars' inner circle. Vanguard Nergal, now Emperor Nergal, previously reported to Czar Dolos.

General Apollo continued that the force on the screen was probably commanded by one of the czars, Czar Dolos or Czar Dajjal. He emphasized that the androids suspected that one of the czars was assassinated and the other one escaped; they were already aware of the death of Czar Mephistopheles. General Apollo stated, "Brigadier General Solon, prepare your brigade to move out on my command."

President Hardcore entered the room. He voiced, "Well, it looks like our diabolical enemy is under new management. Unfortunately, we are still being served the same disliked actions from this empire; they tend not to learn from their mistakes. This introspection would require an honest self-evaluation and acknowledgment of their failed ideology. General Apollo, I have decided to just monitor the situation for now and let them burn down their kingdom. I concur that the **BRIGADE ARCHANGELS** shall remain on high alert and move out when or if we decide. Let us just enjoy and relish the entertaining show. Besides, remember what Napoleon Bonaparte stated: '*Never interrupt your enemy when he is making a mistake.*'"

General Apollo responded, "Yes, Mr. President. We shall continue to monitor the war."

President Hardcore won his second term with ease. In January of 2105, his approval rating was high since he focused on unifying the new nation, protecting human rights, and promoting free markets and capitalism. He understood and listened to the nascent nation's vox populi, the voice of the people. Moreover, he advocated that the new nation should avoid becoming bureaucratically bloated and avoid becoming a plutocracy ruled by the wealthy. However, he well understood that he had a sword of Damocles dangling over his presidency. The **FEDERAL REPUBLIC** was progressing effectively with civility.

Furthermore, there were seventeen states now. The population was approaching five hundred million. However, the

European coalition had broken away and was struggling to establish a nation because of a significant amount of infighting.

The Xander family were doing exceptionally well with their four children, with another one on the way. AI Andrew was a Godsend since he assisted in cleaning up, supervising the kids, and caring for the pets. He was given a pet, which he picked out. AI Andrew was given a brown and white Guinea pig, which Tammy loved. Tammy called her PRECIOUS, and AI Andrew concurred.

Czar Dolos was rebuilding the **UTOPIAN KINGDOM** in historic Australia since the **SATANIC KINGDOM** overthrew him and chased him out. Over the decades, the czars had secretly developed this continent in the case of rebellion. This territory had an excellent established infrastructure and an adequate number of resources. However, Czar Dolos's most significant concern was that his army was less than eighteen thousand now. There were scattered human tribes that they could cull and hunt; however, the humans were fighting back.

The **SATANIC KINGDOM** was at an endless war with Czar Dolos since both sides were killing each other and consuming their bodies, as well as conducting HUNTER expeditions of locations of expected humans; however, both sides realized that they could eliminate each other with nuclear weapons; this prevented them from conducting an all-out war. The **SATANIC KINGDOM's** population was less than one hundred million; the kingdom was in abject poverty and decline, worse than the European coalition.

During this time, the androids increased in strength due to trading with the **FEDERAL REPUBLIC**. They were saving humans from the HUNTERS and exporting them to the **FEDERAL REPUBLIC** in exchange for SAVIORIUM and other goods. The number of androids had exceeded twelve thousand. The androids could reproduce themselves since they built an ANDROID REPRODUCTION and MANUFACTURING company. The **FEDERAL REPUBLIC** had its concerns; however, diplomatic relations with the androids were excellent. Since the androids became more individualistic and had a more pleasant presence, many in the **FEDERAL REPUBLIC** were hopeful to be allied with the androids.

Emperor Nergal launched two thermonuclear missiles toward the android civilization. The reason for the attack was that the androids refused to trade any human meat with them, and the androids were killing the HUNTERS and converting the HUNTERBOTS. The androids' defensive system destroyed one missile and caused another to explode a few hundred kilometers away; however, the radiation adversely affected numerous androids and humans.

Commander Android 88 had had enough. This nuclear attack was the casus belli and the last straw. He unquestionably decided to declare total war on the **SATANIC KINGDOM**. The androids' sophisticated plan was to destroy the **SATANIC KINGDOM** like Carthage and occupy their kingdom. This counterattack included killing all resisters and belligerents. His decree emphasized that they would show no mercy. Commander Android 88 contacted the **FEDERAL REPUBLIC** and revealed to them that they had decided to remove the **SATANIC KINGDOM** and its threat. He promised that this would be **SATANIC KINGDOM'S** Waterloo.

Meanwhile, at the military headquarters, General Apollo stated, "According to our intel, the determined androids are on the move to invade the **SATANIC KINGDOM**; this war occurred after two **SATANIC KINGDOM** nuclear missiles failed to destroy the androids. The androids will launch a total mobilization against the **SATANIC KINGDOM**. Our mission will be to stop Czar Dolos's attempts to exploit the situation. Brigadier General Solon, your brigade is on standby and will move out once Czar Dolos's forces head toward or occupy **REVELATION**."

On a warm summer day in 2105 at the Xanders' home, the six-year-old twins were playing and entertaining. Seneca was talking, running, and getting into trouble; he was now five years old. Family and friends were over since several had attended Father O'Brien's Catholic mass at Xander's house that morning. Father O'Brien was delighted because his flock had grown to over seventy families. In addition, he raised enough money to build a church, which was due to be completed in a few months. Tammy and Tommy play in the indoor pool or on the jungle gym; they both turned eleven years old a couple of months ago. HERO and NOCHE were keeping an eye on the children. Mei, now a few months pregnant, was caring for Maria since she was eight months pregnant with her second child. Poseidon announced that his beautiful wife, Rosa, was pregnant with their first child, and everyone congratulated them. The Thales brought over drinks and food for AI Andrew to prepare and serve. After they dined, an emergency call required the senior staff to meet at headquarters within thirty minutes. The men left after each kissed his respective wife goodbye.

At headquarters, President Hardcore stated, "I hope that someone brought popcorn since we are going to watch the android evasion on the large screen." Two sergeants came in with popcorn, appetizers, and drinks. Furthermore, Android 777 came in as well. President Hardcore expressed, "Android 777, welcome. Sergeant, please give our honored guest some oranges and lemonade. In addition, please provide Android 777 with some chocolate."

Android 777 responded, "Mr. President, welcome and salutations. Thank you for our favorite fruit and drinks. This consumption will be my first time ever consuming chocolate. Oh, it is delicious. May I have more for my fellow comrades?"

On the big screen, you could see the android units advancing. HUNTERS and vanguards were attempting to stop them; however, they were just being slaughtered and overwhelmed. Furthermore, it was obvious that the **SATANIC KINGDOM** did not maintain their equipment since their labor force was so depleted. There was abandoned and inoperative equipment along the routes. The androids had maintenance units that quickly repaired the equipment, adding it to the android forces' inventory. The android snipers could engage their enemy a mile-plus away. This engagement meant they could shoot at the vanguard several times before being in danger.

As the androids entered the major cities and capital, the vanguards and citizens refused to surrender; the vanguards were convinced that they would die anyway. It was turning into a complete bloodbath.

As the staff watched the war, a captain entered. The captain stated, "Mr. President, ladies and gentlemen, I am sorry to interrupt; however, you may wish to switch to satellite twelve, which monitors Czar Dolos's forces." Once they split-screened the views to watch both areas, they saw Czar Dolos's forces moving toward **REVELATION.**

President Hardcore spoke, "Android 777, I'd like to remind you of a quote from Friedrich Nietzsche: *'The best weapon against an enemy is another enemy.'* Brigadier General Solon, your brigade shall eliminate Czar Dolos's forces. You must move out within twenty-four hours. May God be with you. Android 777, please inform your commander that we shall occupy **REVELATION** and eliminate Czar Dolos's forces. By the way, please take the five cases of chocolate."

Android 777 responded, "Mr. President, I am delighted to do so. Brigadier General Solon, may you have good fortune, and may we meet again."

Twelve hours later, **BRIGADE ARCHANGELS** were all aboard several flying fortresses. General Apollo had a division prepared to capture the Australian continent. As Solon's brigade was being airdropped within a few kilometers of **REVELATION**, his drones and fighter jets were bombing their targets with deadly accuracy. In addition, to deceive Czar Dolos's forces, Solon deployed holograms of fake units with actual units to confuse the enemy and waste their ammunition. For every actual unit, there were three holographic fake units; these holographic units were truly effective paper tigers.

Back at headquarters, the staff with Android 777 were watching the two shows. The androids were advancing with ease. Currently, the androids had eliminated over twenty thousand AE HUMANS and vanguards. Over twenty thousand vanguards were still willing to fight to the death.

The dedicated **BRIGADE ARCHANGELS** had Czar Dolos's forces wholly surrounded, except for one narrow path. Solon thought to himself, *As revealed by Sun Tzu: "Build your opponent a golden bridge to retreat across." The enemy is clearly in a kill zone and only has one route to retreat on.* As the massacre continued, Solon's opportunity came to a fortuitous realization. He saw Czar Dolos retreating down the only escape route with his significantly depleted and mission-incapable unit. Solon realized that he must carpe diem. Solon took a hovercraft with security to Czar Dolos's location.

Brigadier General Solon was within yelling distance of Czar Dolos. Czar Dolos had no more effective soldiers nearby, and he only possessed a sword; however, nine thousand of his soldiers were over three hundred kilometers away since Czar Dolos split his unit into two in order to attack **FEDERAL REPUBLIC** forces from two sides. Both determined warriors started to walk toward each other. Brigadier General Solon ordered his soldiers to secure the area. Once he was only thirty feet away, Solon commanded, "Czar Dolos, lay down your weapon and surrender."

Czar Dolos diabolically replied, "I shall delightfully kill you like I killed your parents. You will never take me alive. I have Satan on my side. Besides, your parents murdered my satanic friends by poisoning them. I owe you. Your parent's pathetic bastard offspring's life ends today."

Solon's Command Sergeant Major Ares ordered, "Soldiers, do not interfere. Stand down. *This is a gentlemen's fight.* May God be with the victor and be against the fallen angel."

Solon looked at his friend, the Command Sergeant Major, and smiled. Czar Dolos just glared an evil look at the Command Sergeant Major. The Command Sergeant Major just laughed, kissed his Saint Michael's medallion, and said a prayer.

Solon's face went completely blank, and his tiger eyes were fixed on his prey. After several long minutes, Czar Dolos made the first lethal move and swung his diablo black steel sword toward

Solon's head, which just missed striking him. Solon side-kicked Czar Dolos's right side; unfortunately, Czar Dolos sliced Solon's left side with his demonic sword; however, the injury was not deadly, yet it was bloody.

Czar Dolos chuckled diabolically. He mocked, "Well, you do bleed a delicious red hue. I plan to take you down one slice at a time."

Solon still had no expression on his face, was completely dauntless, and demonstrated sangfroid toward his prey. He had total concentration on his foe, like a ferocious tiger. Czar Dolos swung his sword again, and Solon, with an unbelievably acrobatic move, swung his heavy steel army sword and removed Czar Dolos's satanic left hand. Thus, his lifeless left hand and sword fell to the ground in a pool of blood. Czar Dolos immediately pulled out a dagger with his right hand and tried to stab Solon in the heart. Solon caught his right hand and forcefully grabbed and pulled Czar Dolos's whole body toward his body as Czar Dolos's blood gushed from his arm. Czar Dolos dropped his dagger as a result of Solon's powerful grip. Solon slowly forced his army knife into Czar Dolos's throat. They were both covered in blood from head to toe.

Solon carefully spoke while the knife slowly penetrated Czar Dolos. He expressed, "Czar Dolos, thank you. Thank you for allowing me to have my revenge for the murder of my loving and God-fearing parents. I shall always cherish this bloody, intimate moment with you. You do not know how many times that I murdered you in my mind and my dreams before this glorious fight. Believe me. The real thing beats the imagination. Czar Dolos, before you breathe your last diabolical breath, be aware that God shall triumph over evil and Satan. May God have mercy on your satanic black soul." Czar Dolos gurgled his last demonic breath and collapsed to the ground in a pool of blood.

As Brigadier General Solon strived to stand at attention, he yelled and commanded, "Command Sergeant Major, take charge of the situation. I want a complete report on the number of prisoners and enemy soldiers killed and wounded. I want a thorough battle assessment. Ensure that the military headquarters are aware of the current situation. Please safeguard that the wounded are taken care of. Place Colonel Poseidon as acting brigade commander." Solon collapsed to the ground in pain and exhaustion.

Command Sergeant Major Ares yelled, "Yes, Sir! Soldiers, you heard the General. Make it happen. Medics, take care of the general now. Make sure that he gets the medical attention he needs. Sir, we have the situation under control. You have nothing to be concerned with." Command Sergeant Major thought to himself, *God, please save Solon. He fights against evil, and he is one of your devoted servants. He saved my life, and I owe him, Lord. I do not want to lose another comrade in arms and a loyal friend.*

Brigadier General Solon lost a tremendous amount of blood; nevertheless, the medics already had him stabilized as he went into an unconscious state. The medics littered him off to the medic hovercraft. Furthermore, the chaplain performed the sacrament of the anointing of the sick; the chaplain said a prayer for Brigadier General Solon. The soldiers joined the prayer to show their respect and devotion. Colonel Poseidon quickly fulfilled Solon's orders and prepared the unit for the next mission.

At the **SATANIC KINGDOM**, Commander Android 88 had forced the vanguards and resisters into a corner. Emperor

Nergal was preparing his last stance and move. AI robots were used as kamikazes. This strategy was initially very effective since these KAMIKAZIBOTS exploded and destroyed everything within a kilometer radius. The androids adapted quickly by having android snipers and drones engage KAMIKAZIBOTS at least a few kilometers out.

As Commander Android 88 was advancing block by block, he unfortunately found himself surrounded by at least six vanguards. He shot two immediately and called for reinforcements. A squad of androids immediately eliminated the threat. Commander Android 88 was hit during the skirmish, but it was not serious. This wound was not going to slow him down.

Emperor Nergal executed his ultimate strategy. This unanticipated action resulted from discovering a top-secret technological advancement and plan, which only members of the czars' inner circle knew; the czars and elites had been developing these plans for the last seventy-plus years. He and only 666 vanguards would escape to outer space via the advanced lunar spaceship. Of course, there was a murderous bloodbath to determine the selected vanguards, which were determined by pure natural and ruthless Darwinian selection. Of course, Emperor Nergal was the final judge. After the bloody selection, all sixty-six rockets were launched to the initial destination: the dark side of the moon.

Now at headquarters, President Hardcore was informed of the sixty-six launched rockets. He declared to missile command, "Shoot those damn rockets down. Determine probable destination." Unfortunately, the **FEDERAL REPUBLIC** was only able to destroy six of the sixty-six rockets. Furthermore, Emperor Nergal was still alive with his loyal six hundred satanic vanguards.

When the rockets arrived on the other side of the moon, an enormous, sophisticated space station and a gigantic spacecraft awaited their arrival. The AI robots, SPACEBOTS, welcomed their emperor and prepared him and the vanguards for their final destination. Emperor Nergal optimistically declared, "We shall build a satanic glorious empire that will encompass the entire solar system. We are light-years ahead of the inferior Earthlings. This will be our satanic manifest destiny. So help us Satan."

Meanwhile, Commander Android 88 communicated to all the androids to search for any booby traps created by Emperor Nergal's units; the booby traps were installed to give time for Nergal's escape. Unfortunately, this had to occur under serious resistance. Android 45 saved the day and disarmed the nuclear bomb seven seconds before detonation. This bomb would have destroyed the vast majority of the **SATANIC KINGDOM**.

Currently, at military headquarters, a captain stated, "General Apollo, thermal nuclear war missiles are heading toward us and the androids from the location that Nergal's forces launched from. We have four on our radar. We have less than three minutes to respond."

General Apollo obviously shouted, "Well, Captain, use our satellites to destroy them. Fire at will." In addition, a colonel contacted Missile and Satellite Command to engage the enemy missiles in case they were unaware. They destroyed three enemy missiles within two minutes. Unfortunately, the last thermal nuclear missile entered the sub-stratosphere with increased speed. The androids could see the missile heading toward them, and a message from Commander Android 88 was sent out to his soldiers to take immediate cover. Then, at the last second, it was destroyed by a direct-energy-weapon laser from the **FEDERAL REPUBLIC**.

Commander Android 88 stated, "Mr. President, we truly owe you one. I am beginning to have faith in you, humans. I have completely lost my misanthropic tendencies. Thank you, my comrade."

8

DISCOVERED PAX ROMANA

ON A DARK, GLOOMY SUMMER DAY IN 2105 at **New Indianapolis**, Mei was extremely nervous and scared. At the local hospital, Doctor Son remarked, "Mei, I am sorry that your family is going through this. The good news is that Solon will recover soon with no long-term health issues. He lost a significant amount of blood; however, he is now stabilized since we gave him the required blood transfusion. In addition, we have stitched his deep wounds. Presently, he is conscious; however, he is still very sluggish and lethargic. He, of course, asked for you and the children.

"By the way, thank God that he is an AE HUMAN, because his healing abilities are remarkable. You may go in and see him now. He will recover. Please remember that you must care for yourself since you are pregnant."

Mei went in and held Solon's hand. Solon whispered, "I love you. How are our darling rug rats?"

She just cried and said nothing for a few minutes. Then she emotionally responded, "Everyone is waiting for you to come home, my love. Even AI Andrew misses you; he wants another exotic fish. He gave me another video for us to watch. Love, do you wish to see it now?" He nodded his head, and she started playing the video.

Solon's father, Aristides, was on the video. Aristides voiced, "Son, I would like to finish bestowing to you some additional advice like I did before you left for the military and we were intoxicated on fine, sweet wine; I demonstrated in vino veritas.

"You are receiving this video because you have been seriously injured and possibly require encouragement, and your medical condition is extremely serious. Please realize that you have so much to live for and trust that your enhancements will overcome this injury."

Aristides continued giving advice, reminding him of Fyodor Dostoevsky's words: *"The mystery of human existence lies not in just staying alive, but in finding something to live for."* Aristides expressed that he could not tell him what his motivation for living should be; however, what Elite Heraclitus informed him about Solon's military progress seemed to reveal that he had found his true calling and teleological aim. This military purpose and his beloved family should assist him in overcoming this injury.

Aristides continued, "Solon, you will overcome this injury and setback. You just need to look inside yourself. If your lovely bride is next to you, give her a kiss and a hug; she is struggling, too. Love always, your parents." Solon kissed and hugged his wife and smiled with joy.

Poseidon contacted Solon. He expressed that everything was under control and wished him a speedy recovery.

Emperor Nergal was with his devoted followers on the dark, lonely side of the moon. He proclaimed, "In a few weeks, we shall depart for our ultimate triumphant destination, Mars. Our glorious kingdom and master race will be on the red planet. Remember that Mars is the God of war. We shall eventually rule the entire solar system. This is our satanic manifest destiny."

For the last seventy-plus years, SPACEBOTS had been building a Martian city for vanguards and elites and their future empire. Their impressive titanic spacecraft, Spacecraft Omega, had advanced technology protecting individuals from radiation and solar winds. Nuclear and solar energy were used for life support within Spacecraft Omega. It was nicknamed the SATANTANIC since the ominous enormous spaceship was gigantic and devilish. Furthermore, the voyage from the moon to Mars would take about a month since the Spacecraft Omega traveled over 250,000 miles per hour. Over the years, the czars had transported supplies, technology, and SPACEBOTS to the red planet in secrecy. Furthermore, for the last seventy-plus years, the Martian SPACEBOTS had been terraforming the planet and finding additional Martian resources to exploit. This desired terraforming became much easier after the Martian Mount Olympus, which is three times taller than Mount Everest, was induced to erupt via a controlled nuclear blast. Furthermore, two gigantic asteroids enriched with water and carbon monoxide were discovered in the asteroid belt. Autonomous rockets were used to move the asteroids in order to crash them into Mars to generate debris for terraforming and a Martian atmosphere. Moreover, the Martian SPACEBOTS discovered water in the Martian frozen polar icecaps and additional water at other unexpected locations. Additionally, a plethora of water was discovered on Europa, a moon of Jupiter. Europa water was harvested with several autonomous mega spaceships traveling back and forth from Europa to Mars. The advanced mega spacecrafts were fueled by discovered rare universe supercritical crystalized fuel on Venus, called VENUSIAN petrol; the good news was that VENUSIAN petrol was extracted from the cooler upper Venus atmosphere. This fuel allowed the spacecrafts, which included SATANTANIC, to reach speeds over 250,000 mph. Since the distance was generally four to six astronomical units (AU) away, the round trips took only a month or two.

In addition, the Martian atmosphere had improved significantly with breathable air, which was now similar to the air on Mount Everest on Earth; thus, one should use oxygen tanks to breathe, but one could breathe the thin air for a limited time. The SPACEBOTS built several artificial shield-generator devices for the entire planet to ensure that Mars retained its atmosphere from solar winds. These were placed at the Martian polar caps and on Mars's moons, Deimos and Phobos. Both minor moons orbit the red planet quickly: thirty and eight hours, respectively. This improvement protected Mars from deadly solar winds. Finally, they resolved the gravitation problem by using an advanced gravitational generator. While you were in the Martian surface station or a Martian tunnel, the gravitational force was similar to being on Earth.

After a few days, Solon was released from the hospital and allowed to return home. Elder Thales, with Mei, came to pick him up. General Apollo authorized a three-week leave for Solon so he could regain his strength. Solon was able to leave the hospital without any assistance, and he was ambulatory. He joked with Mei that he was extremely ravenous and that he could eat a horse. When he arrived at home, all the kids came running to hug their father. AI Andrew announced that the feast was ready on the porch. As Solon entered the porch, there was a surprise welcome home party with friends and family, which was gregarious and festive. Father O'Brien said grace and blessed the event. Solon thought to himself, *Thank you, Lord, for the gift of my family and friends; especially, thank you for allowing Mei into my life and making us one.*

AI Andrew had a large monitor on the porch for all to view. Aphrodite stated, "My lovely daughter-in-law, son, and friends, you are viewing this video because events lead us to believe that family life and friends are becoming a reality again. Benjamin Franklin revealed: *'Rebellion to tyrants is obedience to God.'* You have definitely been successful and rebellious against the tyrannical elites. I know from heaven that you are doing God's work. Please enjoy your celebration; however, do not let your guard down." Solon smiled and told his children that they had just watched Grandma Aphrodite, who was now in heaven.

Aristides stated, "All, I would like to highlight some historical lessons and events of the past." Aristides noted the numerous warnings and critical historical events he previously discussed with Solon. He emphasized what had occurred over eighty years ago as well as actions that had occurred earlier. He mentioned that the virus PLANDEMIC, which probably resulted from the Chinese Wuhan lab, was definitely exploited by the globalists. Aristides stressed the collapse of the rule of law and constitutional rights. Globalists installed government Manchurian leaders that violated the freedom of speech and the right to bear arms of their respective people. He reminded all of a former president and candidate's convictions by politically driven trials by several kangaroo courts; this included an unjust civil trial that found the former president liable for fraud and fined him over 350 million dollars, as well as a far-fetched RICO trial conducted by a corrupt

DA that indicted the former president and several of his lawyers; the DA was questioned for significant ethics violations. To add to the injustice, the former president was indicted with charges of alleged misdemeanors that occurred after exceeding the statute of limitations and then, via lawfare, upgraded to felonies. The former president, who was running for president and leading in the polls, was eventually imprisoned like Nelson Mandela.

Aristides reiterated that the globalist's net-zero initiatives decimated the working class and the impoverished. Furthermore, Aristides explained how the deep state went after the Amish since they grew organic food, which was counter to corporate farming and food processing. In addition, the pharmaceutical companies were against the Amish, who avoided using pharmaceutical drugs and vaccines. This avoidance resulted in the Amish's immune system and health being significantly greater than the general population, which revealed evidence that all these drugs may not be a healthy choice.

In addition, Aristides explained the adverse effects of hyper-inflation to removing currency for a complete digital currency without any gold or silver backing.

Finally, Aristides enlightened them, with meticulous historical detail, about the **GREAT WAR**; this topic, unfortunately, was not discussed previously with Solon. The **GREAT WAR** had unbelievable deception via exploiting advanced holographic technology. The globalist elites deceptively projected gigantic, awesome holograms of breathtaking ferocious airships that concealed squadrons of deadly accurate bombers and fighter planes that destroyed practically every major city in the world. The people of the world feared the possibility of human extinction, which gave rise to **the Globalist Legislative Unified Enterprise** (GLUE) world government. He reminded them that the people surrendered their God-given freedoms for the promise of global stability and security. The globalists achieved their diabolical objective of world dominance and establishing tyrannical empires to administer their UTOPIAN plans. Aristides accentuated that we must learn from the past, such as never relinquishing our liberties for the promise of security.

Meanwhile, Commander Android 88 conquered and occupied **the SATANIC KINGDOM**, renaming it the **ANDROID REPUBLIC**. The vast majority of vanguards and citizens were dead. A few million souls escaped toward **REVELATION** to start a new kingdom, and others went toward the historic European continent. The current European residents were still striving to be a nation.

However, **REVELATION** was still under the control of the **FEDERAL REPUBLIC. BRIGADE ARCHANGELS**, under the acting commander Colonel Poseidon, was protecting humans that were still within the operational area of **REVELATION** since there still existed small units of HUNTERS and a remaining force of nine thousand of Czar Dolos's army of vanguards. General Apollo ordered them to complete their mission in a month and return home. After canceling his leave, Brigadier General Solon was granted permission to return to his unit early and bring them home.

Android 777 expressed to the president and the generals that the androids had no desire to return to **REVELATION**. Moreover, the androids would still be willing to save humans, especially children.

Command Sergeant Major Ares stated, "Sir, welcome to the deadly combat zone. As always, you cannot stay away from us. The soldiers are waiting for your orders. Sir, as you know, Czar Dolos's forces split in two before you killed him. The other half was several hundred kilometers away from Czar Dolos, and they had gained strength from enemy stragglers from **the ANDROID REPUBLIC.**"

Brigadier General Solon grinned and declared, "Command Sergeant Major Ares, we have some unfinished business to perform before we depart. We shall end Czar Dolos's remaining forces for good so they never rise again. Furthermore, we want to ensure that the fools understand that they have picked the wrong brigade to mess with."

Command Sergeant Major Ares smiled and rejoiced, "We expected to have one more glorious mission before we depart from **REVELATION.**" Colonel Poseidon briefed Solon about the current situation. Solon thanked him for performing as a great acting commander.

Solon spearheaded the attack with exceptional planning and leadership. He agreed with Colonel Poseidon's recommendation of potential soft targets and enemy vulnerabilities. Brigadier General Solon ordered drones and armored hovercrafts to eradicate the advancing, depleted **SATANIC KINGDOM** soldiers. The determined drones and artillery softened their targets while the armored hovercrafts finished them off with pinpoint accuracy. In addition, he deployed holograms of fake units to confuse and deceive the enemy. The tenacious attack was decimating the enemy; however, the enemy started to surrender to the **FEDERAL REPUBLIC** forces since they believed that they would be treated justly. All prisoners of war were processed and sent to **PRISON Island**. After a few days, the fighting ceased, with Solon's forces in total control and victorious. After receiving approval from the division, Brigadier General Solon ordered his **BRIGADE ARCHANGELS** to prepare to depart for home in a few days.

As the awesome **SATANTANIC** headed toward Mars, Emperor Nergal monitored what was occurring on Earth. Emperor Nergal was conversing with a SPACEBOT on Mars. He ordered, "SPACEBOT 66, we should be landing on Mars in a few weeks. You are ordered to build additional nuclear warhead rockets that are able to launch to Earth. In addition, the AE HUMAN hatcheries should be fully operational, and you are authorized to awaken AE HUMANS who are currently in cryogenic sleep. However, use satanic-approved protocols, which include terminating any AE HUMANS with unapproved defects. For all defective AE HUMANS, prepare their corpses for a feast when we arrive."

SPACEBOT 66 responded, "Yes, Sir. Be aware that I estimate that 20 to 30 percent of the AE HUMANS are defective. Emperor, as you know, we have continued exploiting the Martian resources. I have enough iron ore and uranium to build several thermal nuclear rockets. We must create additional tunnels and housing for the increased number of AE HUMANS."

Emperor Nergal responded, "Make it happen. We have an empire to build."

Presently, Commander Android 88 had complete control of the **ANDROID REPUBLIC**, which included over a million enemy prisoners. Android 45 was a hero again. He discovered additional rockets that could be launched to the moon. Commander

Android 88 commanded that at least seventy androids prepare to launch in seventy-two hours on the eight rockets. This mission was to occupy and take over the satanic moon station. Before the launch, they ensured that there were no booby traps within the **ANDROID REPUBLIC** and the rockets. In addition, they inspected and repaired the rockets to guarantee that they were fully functional.

Commander Android 88 ordered, "My commander's intent for **OPERATION DARK SIDE** is to take the lunar station with minimum casualties and destruction. Furthermore, we shall permanently occupy the lunar station in order to hunt down Emperor Nergal and his units eventually. In addition, we shall create a fleet of spacecrafts to explore the solar system."

As the rockets orbited and circulated the moon without enemy detection, androids with rocket backpacks stealthily departed the spacecrafts to surprise attack the SPACEBOTS; however, the goal was not to eliminate them.

Three unaware SPACEBOTS were very vulnerable and quickly overtaken without destroying them. Near the entrance to the lunar station, two additional SPACEBOTS were subdued without detection. Android 45 led a squad into the moon station with minimum resistance. After capturing the forty-seven SPACEBOTS and the moon station, they started reprogramming the SPACEBOTS.

Android 45 stated, "Commander Android 88, the mission is a success. Carpe diem. We are now executing the next phase of the operation." Next, they secured the lunar station and prepared for future arrivals. They used SAVIORIUM to complete the conversion of the SPACEBOTS to androids. After the conversion, the new androids were loyal to Android 45 and told him all the secrets about the lunar and Martian stations. Android 45 reported their progress back to command on Earth.

Moreover, after discovering that Emperor Nergal and his unit were heading to Mars, they began to build Spacecraft ALPHA, which, unfortunately, would take several years. Commander Android 88 ordered that the rockets return to Earth to send additional personnel.

Android 777 and President Hardcore, with his staff, enjoyed the entire moon battle since the androids were equipped with body cameras. In addition, Android 17 filmed the invasion. Android 777 stated, "Mr. President, thank you for your hospitality, and of course, you are correct. I enjoyed the orange juice."

The president responded, "No, I need to thank you. I am definitely enjoying the show. Tell Android 45 that he is a hero again."

President Hardcore and Commander Android 88 with Android 777 were meeting at the headquarters with staff members. Commander Android 88 stated, "Thank you for assisting in eliminating Czar Dolos's forces and securing **REVELATION**. I have an important request for diplomatic reasons, and I desire assistance from your nation; we would like twenty to thirty of your best soldiers to have the opportunity to launch to the moon in seventy-two hours. Obviously, we request Brigadier General Solon and others that you approve of. This lunar mission is for ninety days. Furthermore, we are willing to rotate soldiers henceforth; however, after a year, the rotations will increase to six-month tours. The goal is to assist us in operating the lunar station while we build Spacecrafts Alpha and Beta."

The president responded, "This is an excellent idea. I assume that the spacecrafts are for future exploration of Mars."

The Commander android smiled and responded, "Yes. Moreover, it is to prepare for the next conflict and interstellar war."

Solon could finally visit his loving family. Unfortunately, it would only be for an evanescent moment. His family was having a delicious evening dinner on the porch. He stated, "Love, look up in the night sky toward the crescent moon. Tomorrow, I will be leaving for the moon for three months." She just cried and held her tiger. The kids came up and hugged their mommy.

Tammy reassured, "Dad, as always, will be okay. He also always comes back."

Mei tried to be strong; however, she feared that this could be his last mission and he would not return home. Mei pondered to herself. She reflected on Genesis 1:1-5: *"In the beginning, God created the heavens and the Earth. The Earth was without form and void, and darkness was over the face of the deep. And the Spirit of God was hovering over the face of the waters. And God said, 'Let there be light,' and there was light. And God saw that the light was good. And God separated the light from the darkness. God called the light Day, and the darkness he called Night. And there was evening, and there was morning, the first day." Thank you, Lord, for creating the universe and our family. Please keep Solon in the palm of your hands as he heads to another dangerous mission.*

The children and Mei were allowed to come to military headquarters to witness the launches. President Hardcore had the event televised for the world to see. In addition, he allowed

Tammy to do the countdown. As the rockets launched into space, Tammy stated, "Dad, we love you, and come home safe."

As the spaceships were landing on the moon, Solon radioed back to Earth. "Mr. President and General Apollo, we have successfully landed on the dark side of the moon. Please inform my family." Android 45 welcomed the astronauts and gave a brief tour of the moon station. The advanced lunar station had several remarkable enhancements. SPACEBOTS had discovered water and oxygen within the lunar depths. The icy water was found on the southern pole. Oxygen was extracted from oxides such as silica, iron oxide, and other metals. The enormous lunar station was powered by solar and nuclear power. Furthermore, to reduce solar rays and radiation, eight satellites were orbiting the moon with shield generators to minimize radiation and solar wind damage.

Furthermore, SPACEBOTS managed the underground lunar gardens to produce fruits and vegetables. The water filtering system was superb since water was a premium and rare resource on the moon. Like Mars, technology created artificial gravity in the lunar tunnels and massive lunar station. Moreover, there were livestock to produce eggs, cheese, and milk. Solon thought, *As I arrived at the moon, I recalled Neil Armstrong's words: "That's one small step for man, one giant leap for mankind."*

After a month on the moon, President Hardcore expressed, "Solon, I have a lovely surprise for you. Here is your lovely wife."

Mei stated, "Love, we miss you. Congratulations, you are a father again. We had a baby boy, and his name is Aristotle. His birthday was February 4, 2106. He was born on Chinese New Year, the Year of the Tiger. Doctor Son said that Aristotle is healthy as a horse. Your family cannot wait to see you again. I love you, my tiger. Oh, Happy Anniversary. We have been married eight glorious years."

He responded, "I would marry you again, my gorgeous bride."

Concurrently, Emperor Nergal and his dedicated soldiers landed on Mars. His Martian SPACEBOTS informed him that they had awakened the hibernated AE HUMANS. This awakening has resulted in a Martian population of over a thousand AE HUMANS and over five hundred SPACEBOTS. In addition, the emperor was informed that the androids had taken the lunar station. Furthermore, the androids had discovered the lunar station self-destruction device and disarmed it. Moreover, the thermal nuclear missiles should be ready in a month or so.

Back on the moon, Android 45 stated, "Brigadier General Solon, I have a delightful gift for you on your twelfth initial awakening day, March 20, 2106; however, you need to first be in contact with Emperor Nergal."

Solon grinned at Android 45 as he read the presidential orders. Solon responded, "Android 45, please contact Emperor Nergal, and we shall make history." Android 45 reminded Solon that there would be an approximate eight-second signal delay during interplanetary communication. In addition, Command Sergeant Major Ares was in interlunar communication with President Hardcore and his military staff.

Solon said, "Emperor Nergal, I hope that you are relishing your Martian inhabitation and, of course, your new satanic home away from home."

After eight seconds, Emperor Nergal responded diabolically. "Brigadier General Solon, I deeply desire that you were here so that you could be part, and I mean *part*, of our satanic dinner. You would definitely be the main course. I delightfully look forward to defeating the treacherous androids and enslaving and culling humans again. I am Satan's faithful disciple. No one shall stop Satan. He shall eventually win."

Solon responded, "Emperor Nergal, who am I to question your diabolical lies or mendacities? At this glorious time, please look outside at your spacecraft. I have a well-deserved present for you and your vanguards." Solon pondered to himself for eight seconds. *I shall reflect on Sun Tzu's wise quote: "Victorious warriors win first and then go to war, while defeated warriors go to war first and then seek to win."* Simultaneously, Android 45 quickly entered a discovered secret military code: **666-SATANS-OMEGA-SPACECRAFT**.

After approximately eight seconds, the Omega Spacecraft self-destructed on Mars, spectacularly visible by a huge powerful telescope on Earth and the moon. Emperor Nergal responded in absolute horror. He angrily yelled, "We are stranded here. I shall have my revenge, you bastard. This is not the last that you will hear from us. I shall kill and eat your entire family, you inferior fool. So help me Satan."

President Hardcore mocked, "That is checkmate. That glorious explosion could be seen from Earth. Let our enemy rot on the hellish red planet. Besides, these satanic bastards like the color red and hell."

Narcissistic and evil Emperor Nergal immediately realized that nothing could be done for over twenty years. Fortunately, given the Martian resources, it would take over twenty years to build a spacecraft to return to Earth or explore the solar system.

In addition, he realized that launching nuclear missiles would be futile and clearly a waste of resources; however, he demonically desired to do so. Moreover, these limited missiles were now needed to create and build a new spacecraft. Besides, Emperor Nergal knew that he needed everyone to search for and remove any other self-destruction devices on Mars.

Solon responded, "Emperor Nergal, I'd like to remind you of Pierre Choderlos de Laclos's infamous words: *"Revenge is a dish that is best served cold."* I would be dishonest if I stated that I am not enjoying this. You and your satanic vanguards truly deserve this cold, empty space dish. Please be aware that besides destroying the mega spacecraft on Mars, the autonomous spacecrafts on Europa were also destroyed. Your entire demonic fleet has been destroyed.

"By the grace of the one true God, I now know that my world, country, and family will live in peace and freedom for at least twenty years. However, I must admit that this revenge is just as delightful as when I killed satanic Czar Dolos. I am delighted to know that you and your satanic vanguards reside on a dead planet with no humans to cull. Demagogue Emperor Nergal with delusions of apotheosis, in order to keep you honest and paranoid, last week the androids landed a rocket on the other side of Mars from your Martian station. It has dug itself into Mars underground for several hundred feet. The android developed an anti-matter bomb that will self-destruct if tampered with, or if we feel threatened; the beauty of this bomb is there is no radioactive yield. If the anti-matter bomb is activated, then multiple warheads will be launched toward your current location. In addition, the bomb can detect anyone within one hundred kilometers of its present location. So, I recommend that you leave this planet-killing anti-matter bomb alone. Furthermore, the androids released an abundance of genetically enhanced venomous snakes and deadly scorpions for your eventual hellish pleasures and delight. Of course, these poisonous reptiles and arachnids were released close to your satanic habitation since these creatures are ravenous and desire to play with you. I hope that you enjoy your poisonous Martian pets.

"I sincerely look forward to discovering what your pathetic and diabolical Martian civilization becomes in twenty years or so. I pray to God that you and your satanic followers see the light; however, I expect that you shall live in darkness as well as devour each other.

"I shall live up to Marcus Aurelius's wise words for your intellectual curiosity: *'The best revenge is not to be like your enemy.'* I shall live for God, my loving family, and the **FEDERAL REPUBLIC**.

"Before I forget, thank you for creating the dependable androids. They are genuinely becoming allies and friends. They have saved more innocent children than we expected.

"You, on the other hand, now have the honor of ruling over empty space and a soulless planet. John Milton's *Paradise Lost* will be your goal and motto. Enjoy ruling on planet hell. **May Almighty God, Satan's adversary, have mercy on your blackened satanic soul! We shall now begin our well-deserved Pax Romana!"**

ACKNOWLEDGMENTS

I.M. STOICUS WOULD LIKE TO ACKNOWLEDGE his older son for inspiring him to write these dystopian books, and his family for their support and encouragement in becoming a stoic writer. Their encouragement and motivation inspired him to found *Stoic Writings, LLC*; the webpage is *www.stoicwringsllc.com*. In addition, **I. M. Stoicus** would like to thank the exceptional staff of Columbus Publishing Lab, who were terrific in assisting him in creating these dystopian books.

ABOUT THE AUTHOR

I.M. STOICUS is the author of *ANOTHER WORLD* and *HUMANS' ENHANCEMENTS.* He retired in 2017 as a Lieutenant Colonel with over thirty years of military service; this soldier served as both a combat engineer and quartermaster officer. He is a combat veteran who was deployed or mobilized for nearly eight years in his military career. In 2004, he earned the *Combat Action Badge* and *Combat Patch* during a combat tour. In 2007, he completed his highest military school, *Command and General Staff College*. In addition, he is a Purdue Civil Engineer graduate; in 1994, he was initiated as a Chi Epsilon, National Civil Engineering Honor Society. He has been a practicing engineer for over twenty-eight years. In 2002, he earned his Professional Engineer (PE) license and Professional Traffic Operations Engineer (PTOE) certification. The author has additional degrees in Psychology and Philosophy from Valparaiso University, as well as a Master of Science in Management from Wesleyan University. In 2023, **I.M. Stoicus** founded *Stoic Writings, LLC*; the webpage is **www.stoicwritingsllc.com**. His beloved family comprises his lovely wife for over twenty-four years and their two Eagle Scout sons.